Kittens in Crisis

Tabby

Illustratio

Cats in the Caravan

Illustrations by Ann Baum

LUCY DANIELS

A division of Hachette Children's Books

This bind-up edition published in 2011 by Hodder Children's Books

Special thanks to Linda Chapman
Thanks also to C. J. Hall, B.Vet.Med., M.R.C.V.S., for reviewing the veterinary information contained in this book.

First published as a single volume in Great Britain in 1999 by Hodder Children's Books

First published as a single volume in Great Britain in 2001 by Hodder Children's Books

Created by Working Partners Limited, London WC1X 9HH
Original series created by Ben M. Baglio

1

A Catalogue record for this book is available from the British Library

ISBN 978 1 444 90728 5

Typeset in Baskerville by Avon DataSet Ltd, Bidford-on-Avon, Warwickshire

Printed and bound in Great Britain by
CPI Bookmarque Ltd, Croydon, Surrey

The paper and board used in this paperback by Hodder Children's Books are natural recyclable products made from wood grown in sustainable forests. The manufacturing processes conform to the environmental regulations of the country of origin.

Hodder Children's Books
A division of Hachette Children's Books
338 Euston Road, London NW1 3BH
An Hachette UK company
www.hachette.co.uk

rubbed her head against Mandy's chin. She wasn't hurt, just rather surprised at having such an unexpected cuddle. 'Oh, thank goodness!' Mandy whispered, hugging her close.

Suddenly she remembered James and looked across the road.

He was gingerly disentangling himself from his bike. 'Are you all right?' Mandy asked, hurrying over.

'I think so,' said James, pushing his glasses firmly back on to his nose. He looked anxiously at the cat in Mandy's arms. 'How is she?'

'OK, I think,' Mandy said, stroking the cat's soft white fur. 'It's Delilah. You know – she belongs to Mr Ward.'

James nodded and stroked the cat's head. Bill Ward was the village postman. They often passed him doing his rounds on their way to school. 'He brought her in to Animal Ark a couple of weeks ago for a check-up on her pregnancy,' Mandy said. Delilah looked up at her and purred.

'When are her kittens due?' James asked, wheeling his bike off the road.

'In about two weeks, I think,' said Mandy. She looked round at the row of pretty grey stone cottages that nestled together, with sloping

waiting for Mandy's answer he put his head down, his brown hair flopping over his face, and started to pedal like mad.

'That's not fair!' Mandy protested, pedalling furiously after him.

As James sped past the first house, Mandy's sharp eyes noticed a cat coming out of one of the cottage gates just ahead of him. It was a white Persian cat. A very pregnant, white Persian cat who was heading straight towards the road.

James's eyes were looking down as he tried to make the most of his head start.

'James!' Mandy yelled. 'Look out!'

The cat stepped out, her head held high. Her large, cumbersome body swayed as she walked.

'Stop!' cried Mandy in horror.

At the very last moment, James saw the cat. He jammed on his brakes and his bike skewed violently to one side, missing the cat by centimetres.

James and the bike crashed to the ground.

Mandy screeched to a halt and flung her bike on to the pavement. She raced over to the cat and scooped her up. Was she all right? Were there any signs of shock? The cat's rough tongue flicked over Mandy's hand and she

One

Mandy Hope and James Hunter cycled out of Welford village. Daffodils nodded in the spring sunshine as they passed. 'I've got a biology test today,' Mandy groaned. 'I looked over it for two hours last night and I still haven't learned it.'

Mandy knew that if she wanted to be a vet then she had to do well in school, but she hated revising for tests. There were always so many other things that she would rather be doing – like looking after the animals that came into Animal Ark, her parents' veterinary practice.

'You'll do fine,' James, her best friend, reassured her. They approached the last row of houses. 'Race you up the hill!' he called. Not

Tabby in the Tub

roofs and tiny windows. 'We can't leave her out here. Shall we see if Mrs Ward is in?'

'Which cottage is it?' James asked.

Mandy nodded towards a cottage near the end of the row. 'The one with the pink cherry tree in the garden.'

Each of the cottages had a front garden bordered by a privet hedge. James pushed open the wooden gate that led into the Wards' garden. The spring breeze sent fluffy pieces of pale-pink cherry blossom swirling around Mandy's head. Two terracotta pots stood by the front door, purple and white pansies spilling out of them. James reached the door and knocked loudly. A dog barked inside and they heard footsteps approaching.

'Back, Tara!' said a voice inside, and Jane Ward, the postman's wife, opened the door. She was dressed in jeans and a sweatshirt. A black-and-tan dog, about the size of a small Labrador, attempted to wriggle past her but she caught its collar quickly. 'Steady, Tara.' As she caught sight of Delilah in Mandy's arms, her inquiring look changed to one of surprise. 'Delilah! How did you get outside?'

'We found her crossing the road,' Mandy explained.

'I almost ran her over,' admitted James, rather shamefaced.

'But we think she's all right,' said Mandy quickly, seeing a look of concern cross Mrs Ward's face. 'James didn't touch her.'

'I must have forgotten to lock the cat-flap,' groaned Jane, running a hand through her curly blonde hair. 'Thank you so much for bringing her back in. I've been trying to keep her in the house unless I'm outside to keep an eye on her. Her road sense has been terrible since she got pregnant.'

Tara, the dog, was still struggling to greet Mandy and James. Giving up the battle, Jane released her hold on the collar and Tara bounded out joyfully.

James grabbed her just in time to stop her jumping up at Mandy and Delilah. 'Whoa, Tara!' The dog licked his face and hands ecstatically. She was an Australian cattle dog, square-shaped, strong and sturdy with a head a bit like a German shepherd's. James and Mandy had first met Tara when she was just a few months old, and the Wards had bought her to keep Delilah company. Her heavy tail thwacked against James's legs. 'She's as lively as always!' said James with a grin.

Jane smiled and took Delilah from Mandy. 'It's certainly quite a job keeping an eye on both of them.' She put Delilah down and sighed as the cat stalked slowly towards the kitchen. 'I don't know what I'm going to do with Delilah. She's never been good with traffic but she's been ten times worse since she's been pregnant.'

'Just like Duchess,' said Mandy, remembering. 'She got hit by a car when *she* was pregnant.' Duchess was Delilah's mother. The accident had caused her to go into premature labour – luckily both Duchess and all her kittens had survived. She belonged to Richard Tanner, one of Mandy and James's friends in the village. James let Tara go and the happy dog bounced over to Mandy to say hello. Mandy bent down to fuss her and received a lick on the nose. Mandy grinned and scratched Tara's ears. 'How are you going to like the kittens, Tara?'

Jane raised her eyebrows. 'We hope she's going to get on fine with them but we'll keep her away from them at first, at least until they're old enough to cope with her bounciness. We were going to ask your dad about the best way to introduce them. Bill's planning to bring Delilah to the surgery for another check-up tonight.'

'Oh good,' said Mandy, straightening up and looking pleased. 'I'll see her then.'

Jane nodded. 'And you must both come and see the kittens when they are born. It's good for kittens to have visitors.' She smiled. 'Anyway, I'd better let you two get off to school or you'll be late. Thanks again.' She called to Tara. The dog bounded happily inside.

Mandy and James turned back down the path and the door shut behind them. 'Well, that turned out all right,' said James, relieved. 'Now I've just got to see if my bike's still working.'

Mandy nodded but she was only half listening. A slight movement in the hedge had caught her eye. What was it? It looked like an animal. She frowned.

'Earth to Mandy!' said James, waving a hand in front of her face.

Mandy brushed him away and stopped. 'Look,' she said, in a low voice. 'Over there in the hedge. It's a cat.'

James frowned. 'Where? I can't see anything.'

'There,' Mandy insisted, pointing.

James peered at the hedge. A short-haired tabby cat was lying watching them. Her brown-and-black fur blended in perfectly with the shadows. Her ears twitched warily. Her sleek, round body was tense.

Mandy held out her hand and approached quietly. 'Here, puss. There's a good cat.' She wondered what the cat was doing in the Wards' garden and why it looked so nervous. The cat crouched even further into the ground. Now she was closer, Mandy could see that the cat's left ear was torn. Dark clots of dried blood were caked round the nasty wound. Mandy edged closer but it was too close for the cat. Leaping up, it raced across the grass and scrambled clumsily through the far hedge.

'Oh,' said Mandy, watching it go.

James came over. 'Do you know who it belongs to?'

Mandy shook her head. 'I've never seen it before.'

'An animal you don't know!' said James, grinning. 'A miracle!'

Mandy didn't grin back. Her blue eyes looked rather worried. 'Did you see its ear? It was torn. I think it's a stray.'

'It can't be a stray,' James argued. 'It looked fat. It probably belongs to someone new in the village,' he continued. 'That's why you haven't seen it before.'

'But why did it run away like that?' As they reached the road Mandy looked in the direction the cat had gone.

'Oh no!' James said, recognising the look on Mandy's face. 'You're not going after her. We're going to be late enough for school as it is!'

There was no sign of the little tabby cat so, rather reluctantly, Mandy picked up her bike. James's bike had survived the crash with only a few scrapes on the paintwork and a dent in the bell. They cycled off. James chatted away but Mandy was quiet almost all the way. She was thinking about the cat.

James was right, it had looked well-fed. But if it belonged to someone then why hadn't they done something about its ear and why had it looked so nervous? For some reason, she couldn't get the picture of the little cat scrambling through the hedge out of her mind. Something bothered her. It wasn't just its torn ear or the nervous look in its eyes. It was something else. But try as she might she couldn't figure out quite what.

Mandy slowed down as she and James cycled back past the Wards' house on their way home from school, her eyes sweeping across the neat hedges and gardens.

'It's probably sitting safe and sound at home,' said James, glancing at her. Mandy looked at him in surprise. He grinned. 'You were looking for the tabby cat, weren't you?'

Mandy returned the grin. James knew her so well, sometimes it was as though he could read her thoughts. 'But what if it hasn't got a home?'

'If it was a stray it would have been skinnier,' James pointed out.

Mandy nodded, but deep down she still wasn't convinced. They cycled on until they reached the point in the village where they separated. 'See you tomorrow!' she called.

A few minutes later, she turned up the driveway that led to Animal Ark. The veterinary surgery was a modern extension at the back of the old stone cottage where the Hopes lived. Leaving her bike leaning against the surgery wall, Mandy went into the waiting-room.

Jean Knox, the Animal Ark receptionist, was sitting behind the desk. Her glasses dangled on a chain as she poked cautiously at the computer keyboard. 'How was school?' she asked, looking up as Mandy came in.

'OK,' Mandy replied. She frowned. 'Jean, do

you know if anyone's moved into the village with a brown tabby cat?'

Jean shook her head and started tapping with one finger on the keyboard again. 'I haven't heard of anyone. Why?'

Mandy explained. 'It didn't look thin but it had a torn ear and wouldn't come near me.'

Simon, the practice nurse, came out of one of the treatment rooms. He had been at Animal Ark since leaving college and was good friends with Mandy. She asked him the same question.

He thought for a moment but then shook his head. 'Can't help you, I'm afraid,' he said, running a hand through his short blond hair. 'Maybe your mum or dad will know?'

'Where are they?' Mandy asked Jean as Simon returned to the treatment room with a worming powder.

'Your mum's out on a farm visit and your dad's with Mrs Platt,' Jean informed her.

'Antonia's all right, isn't she?' Mandy asked. She was very fond of Mrs Platt's little grey poodle.

Jean nodded. 'Just in for her kennel cough vaccination and some wormer.'

The surgery door opened and in walked Bill Ward, carrying a wicker cat basket. Mandy hurried over. 'Hi! How's Delilah?'

The postman smiled. 'She's grand,' he said, putting the basket down on one of the seats. 'Jane told me about you and James this morning.' He nodded. 'Thanks, love.'

'That's all right,' said Mandy. 'As long as she's safe.'

'Sounds interesting,' said a deep, warm voice. Mandy swung round. Her father had come through from the treatment room with Mrs Platt and was listening to the conversation. His mouth crinkled at the corners under his beard. 'What have you been up to now?'

Mandy told him about the near-accident that morning.

'Delilah's a devil for crossing that road,' Bill Ward said to Mr Hope.

'Bring her in,' said Mr Hope with a smile. He looked at Mandy. 'Are you coming in too?'

'Yes, please.'

Now she was twelve, Mandy was allowed to help with the animals that came in to the surgery. She cleaned out the cages, helped with the medication and assisted in the treatment room. It could be hard work but she loved it. She took her white coat down off the peg and, buttoning it up, hurried to join her dad and Mr

Ward in the treatment room. Delilah was sitting on the rubber-topped table.

Mr Hope ran his hands gently over her bulging sides. 'Not long to go now,' he said, looking up at Bill Ward. 'Have you got her a nesting box?'

Bill nodded, his green eyes serious. 'Just a cardboard box with a lid. It's all ready in the sitting-room and she's been going in and ripping up the newspaper we put inside.' He stroked Delilah's head and looked down fondly at her. 'We're looking forward to these kittens.'

'Excellent,' said Mr Hope. He looked in Delilah's eyes and mouth and then parted the dense white hair on her back and inspected the skin. 'No sign of fleas,' he said. 'But make sure you comb her daily. Can you pass me the thermometer, please, Mandy?'

Mandy held Delilah while her father took Delilah's temperature and then listened to her heart. 'Yes, everything seems normal,' he said. 'She's in fine condition, Bill.'

'She should be,' said Bill Ward. 'She's on four meals a day, best minced chicken; fish and liver twice a week. We've got to keep up her strength.' Carefully, he put Delilah back into her basket.

Mandy helped him to do up the straps. She

wondered if he knew anything about the tabby cat in his garden. 'When James and I were at your house this morning we saw another cat in your garden,' she said. 'It was a tabby cat. Do you know if it belongs to anyone?'

'Aye, I know the one you mean. I'm pretty sure she's a stray.' Bill Ward said as Mr Hope reached for the disinfectant spray and started to wipe down the table ready for the next animal. 'I've caught sight of her a few times. Yesterday, I came out on my way to work and found her lying under the cherry tree. Seeing her condition I tried to catch her but she was off like a shot as soon as I got near.'

'Condition? You mean her ear?' frowned Mandy. 'Yes, I was worried about that.'

Bill looked surprised. 'Ear? Her ears looked OK yesterday.' He shook his head. 'No, I mean about her being pregnant.'

'Pregnant!' Mandy stared.

'Aye. As soon as I saw her I could tell. She was like Delilah, licking her flanks with her belly bulging in just the same way. I'd recognise those signs anywhere at the moment.'

Mandy's blue eyes widened as she realised what had been bothering her. James had said the cat looked fat but the fat had been all to the side and underneath. She thought of the clumsy way the cat had pushed through the hedge. It wasn't well-fed – it was pregnant!

She turned anxiously to her father. 'Do you think she'll be all right?'

Mr Hope scratched his beard. 'Cats normally have kittens without too much problem. But we should probably catch her and take her up to the Animal Sanctuary. She may need feeding up and then there'll be kittens who need homes.'

Bill Ward nodded. 'I put some food out after she ran off. She doesn't look like she's had much to eat recently.'

Mandy was very concerned. She knew that it got harder for female cats to hunt when they were pregnant. The poor thing was probably half starving. She remembered the way its big green eyes had stared at her. 'When can we go, Dad?'

'I've got appointments for the rest of the day,' Mr Hope said. 'And then I'm on call.' He turned to Bill. 'You said you usually see her in the morning?'

The other man nodded.

'Well, would it be all right if we came to your house to see if she's there? If she is, we can catch her and take her to the Animal Sanctuary.'

'Of course, but it will have to be early,' said Bill. 'I start my post-round at seven.'

'So if we come about six o'clock?' Mr Hope suggested.

'Aye, I'll be there,' said Bill. 'I don't rate your chances of catching her though,' he said, scratching his head. 'Not the way she ran off when I tried to get near.'

Two

'Well, here we are,' said Mr Hope, drawing the Land-rover up outside the Wards' house the following morning. 'Now, let's see if we can find this cat.'

Mandy opened the back of the Land-rover. *I hope she's here,* she thought as she lifted out a plastic cat carrier and a bowl of food. She frowned. What would they do if she wasn't?

She joined her father at the Wards' garden gate. The grass was heavy with dew, each blade sparkling in the rays of the early morning sun. Mr Hope scratched his beard. 'I can't see her.'

Mandy's eyes searched the hedges and borders but there was no sign of the cat. Her heart sank. 'Maybe Mr Ward has seen her,' she suggested. 'She might have been here and left already.'

She was halfway down the path towards the front door when she suddenly froze. 'There!' she gasped in a low voice. 'Dad! Look! By the shed!'

The tabby cat lay in the mottled shadows of Bill Ward's garden shed, her brown-and-black coat providing the perfect camouflage. Now, Mandy could see how thin she really was. Her tummy bulged, but her face was gaunt and her backbone stuck out.

'She certainly looks pregnant,' said Mr Hope, quietly coming up behind Mandy. 'Let's see if we can get near.' He took a couple of steps towards the cat. Her ears pricked. Her green eyes widened. 'Put the food down, Mandy,' Mr Hope said softly. Mandy took a step closer and reached out with the bowl but the movement was too much for the cat. Turning on the spot she raced round the side of the cottage.

Mandy saw the concern on her father's face. 'I think Bill was right. This isn't going to be easy,' he said. 'Let's give her time to settle down and then try again. Leave the food here, love. We'll see if Bill minds us watching from inside.'

They walked up to the front door. Bill opened

it. He had seen everything from the sitting-room window. 'Jane's still in bed,' he said. 'But come and have a cup of tea whilst you wait,' he said. 'Watch out for Tara,' he warned, pausing before opening the kitchen door. 'She may jump up.'

As soon as the door was opened Tara flew at them like a canine cannonball. Mandy was thoroughly licked. Mr Hope fended the dog off and when she had stopped jumping up bent down to pat her. 'Mad dog!' he laughed.

Delilah was curled up on one of the pine chairs, oblivious to the commotion. Mandy stroked her. She could feel the bulge of the kittens underneath the Persian's soft, dense fur. She looked so healthy. Mandy couldn't help thinking about the poor little cat outside who had no one to love her or take care of her.

They took mugs of tea into the sitting-room where they could watch the front garden and the food bowl. Delilah lazily followed them through. She lay down and rolled on the rug, stretching herself out and arching her back luxuriantly. Tara sat down, leaning against Mr Hope's legs and looking up at him with dark brown eyes that demanded attention.

'Is that Delilah's nesting box?' asked Mandy,

pointing to a large cardboard box that stood by the radiator.

Bill nodded.

Mandy lifted the lid and looked inside. There was torn-up newspaper and soft paper towels lining the bottom. At the front, Mr Ward had cut a little door for Delilah to get in and out. 'Will you take the lid off when she's having the kittens?' Mandy asked.

Bill nodded. 'We'll keep a watchful eye on her.'

'Now, ring the surgery when she starts, won't you?' said Mr Hope. 'Persians can sometimes have problems giving birth because the kittens have quite large heads. I'd like to be here just to check that everything is OK.'

Mandy glanced out of the window. The tabby cat was creeping cautiously across the lawn, her wary eyes looking from side to side as she approached the bowl of food. 'Dad! It's the cat!'

Mr Hope stood up and looked out of the window. 'I'll go out of the back door,' he said. 'Mandy, you go out of the front. Careful now, remember it's very important that we don't upset her. The kittens would probably be too young to survive if she gave birth now.'

Her heart beating fast, Mandy opened the front door. The cat looked at her and then, putting its head down, carried on eating, gulping the food as fast as she could.

Mandy started to walk slowly towards it, her feet making prints in the dew. Out of the corner of her eye she could see her dad coming up from the other direction. He was crouching down and holding a tasty treat. Mandy edged closer.

The cat stopped eating.

'There now,' Mandy soothed. 'We're not going to hurt you. It's all right.'

The cat turned to run but came face to face with Mr Hope holding out the treat. For one hope-filled moment, Mandy thought the little cat was going to be tempted by the titbit but the next instant the tabby had changed her mind and, swerving across the grass, scrambled away through the hedge.

Mandy watched in dismay. 'Now what are we going to do?'

Mr Hope sighed and heaved himself up off the grass. 'Give up,' he said, wiping the grass off his trousers.

Mandy stared at him in horror. 'Dad, we can't! You saw how thin the poor thing was. She needs looking after!'

Mr Hope put his hand gently on Mandy's shoulder. 'We can't risk upsetting her any more,

Mandy,' he said. 'We'd be putting the unborn kittens in danger.' Mr Hope turned to Bill Ward. 'She seems to have taken a fancy to your garden. If she comes back do you think you can leave some food out for her first thing in the morning and last thing at night? I think we'll have to try to win her trust and hope that, after a few days, she'll let us get close enough to help.'

Bill Ward nodded. 'No problem.'

Relief overwhelmed Mandy. She gave her dad a hug. She should have known he wouldn't let her down. 'Can I help?' she asked eagerly.

'Well, if Bill doesn't object,' Mr Hope said, glancing inquiringly in Bill's direction, 'I suggest that you and James come and leave some food for the cat each day on your way to and from school.'

'It's fine by me,' said Bill cheerfully.

Mandy's blue eyes shone. 'We can wait while she eats,' she said eagerly. 'If she sees us here and realises we're not going to hurt her, maybe, after a bit, she'll let us go up to her.'

Mr Hope raised his eyebrows. 'That sounds like an ideal excuse for being late for school, Mandy Hope.'

'We'll get here early,' promised Mandy. 'We'll be here by seven.'

Mr Hope's eyes twinkled. 'And what will James say about that?'

Mandy grinned. Her dad knew how much James hated getting up early. 'He'll moan at first but he won't really mind. You'll see!'

'Seven o'clock!' exclaimed James as they cycled to school. 'That means getting up at . . .' he did a rapid calculation in his head, '. . . at quarter past *six*!' He stared at Mandy incredulously.

'It's not for long,' said Mandy. 'Just till the cat starts letting us near her.'

'Well, I guess it is in a good cause,' James grumbled.

'You know it is,' said Mandy. Her head was buzzing with excitement. In her schoolbag was a tin of cat food, a fork, a bowl, and some vitamin tablets that her father had given her before she left Animal Ark. 'She's bound to get used to us if we're there when she's eating and then we'll be able to catch her and take care of her.'

'When do you think she'll have her kittens?' asked James. 'She's not quite as big as Delilah yet, is she?'

'But she hasn't had all the food Delilah's had,' Mandy pointed out. 'And anyway Delilah will look larger because of her fluffy hair. Maybe the kittens will be due quite soon.' She frowned. 'I wonder where she's come from? Maybe we should put up some notices.'

James nodded. 'We could ask if we could do them on the school computer at lunch-time and put them up on the way home.'

After school, they took the notices they had printed out round some of the shops in Walton. 'We can do the ones in Welford after we've fed the cat,' said Mandy as they came out of the Walton newsagent's. There's the post office and Animal Ark, of course, and maybe Mr Hardy would let us put one up in the Fox and Goose.'

The wind whipped about their faces as they cycled home. It was a cold day but Mandy hardly noticed. Her mind was fixed on the cat. Would she be in the Wards' garden? Mandy pedalled extra quickly up the last hill, freewheeling down it and screeching to a stop outside the Wards' house. James stopped beside her a few seconds later.

'I'm glad we don't have cats to feed every day!' he gasped, pushing his hair out of his eyes and readjusting his glasses.

Mandy grinned. 'You know you want to see if she's there just as much as I do. Come on!'

As they unlatched the garden gate, Mrs Ward came hurrying out of the front door. 'I'm just popping into Walton,' she said to them. 'Bill told me about the poor little thing,' she said. 'Fancy it being pregnant like Delilah.'

'Have you seen her today?' Mandy asked.

'She was by the shed when I got back from work about ten minutes ago,' Mrs Ward said. 'I put some water out for her. I've been keeping Tara in the back garden so as not to disturb her.'

Mandy and James put down their bags. 'We'll put the food in the same place,' said Mandy. James got out the bowl from Mandy's rucksack and Mandy forked the food out into it. There was no sign of the cat. They sat down in the front porch and watched. Mandy shivered in the cold air and pulled her coat round her.

'There!' whispered James, nudging her gently with his elbow. 'Look!' The tabby cat came slinking along under the cover of the hedge. She edged towards the food, took a nervous look around and plunged her head into the bowl. Her sides moved in and out as she gulped the food down. 'Look how her ribs stick out!' Mandy said.

At the sound of Mandy's voice the cat's head shot up. Her green eyes stared warily in the direction of the porch. Mandy froze. Oh no, why had she spoken? She held her breath. There was a long pause and then the cat slowly lowered her head and continued to devour the food.

The breath rushed out of Mandy. She exchanged relieved looks with James but neither of them dared say another word until the cat had finished and trotted off across the garden and under the hedge.

As they washed the bowl at the outside tap, James said, 'We should bring her some milk. Eric loves milk.' Eric was James's young cat.

Mandy looked a bit doubtful. 'Some adult cats are allergic to cow's milk,' she said, remembering an article she had read in one of her dad's magazines. 'It can give them really bad diarrhoea.' She frowned. 'But pregnant cats need calcium and milk is a really good source. Maybe we *should* give it a try.' Her eyes suddenly brightened. 'I've had an idea! The article said that cats that are allergic to cow's milk can normally drink goat's milk.'

James looked at her. 'Lydia!' he exclaimed.

'Exactly!' said Mandy with a grin.

Lydia Fawcett kept goats at High Cross Farm,

a small farm set up on the hills outside the village. She was great friends with Mandy and James and would be sure to let them have some of her goats' milk.

Throwing the bowl and vitamin tablets into Mandy's rucksack, the two friends set off on their bikes for High Cross Farm. It was a long climb uphill, past the iron gates of Beacon House where the Parker-Smythes lived, past the tall yew hedges that hid Upper Welford Hall, and then a bumpy ride along an unmade lane. They finally reached the new five-barred gate that marked the entrance to High Cross Farm. Pushing it open they wheeled their bikes up the path to the stone farmhouse.

'It's all looking much smarter than it used to,' said James, looking at the freshly painted red door of the house and the recently repaired outbuildings.

'It must be from all the money that the milk's bringing in,' said Mandy, pleased. At one time, Lydia had been very hard up but Mandy and James had helped her to make a profit from the farm by persuading local health food shops to buy Lydia's goats' milk and cheese.

Lydia Fawcett came marching round the side of the barn. She was dressed in old wellies and a tattered jacket. Her weather-beaten face crinkled into a smile when she saw Mandy and James. 'Why, this is a nice surprise,' she said, striding over. 'What brings the pair of you up here? Have you just come to see the goats or are you here for something in particular?'

Mandy explained about the tabby cat and their attempts to feed her up. 'So you see,' she concluded, 'we thought goats' milk might be good for her.'

'It'll be just the thing,' said Lydia, nodding approvingly. 'Best milk in the world.'

'Particularly from High Cross Farm goats,' said James with a grin.

Lydia jerked her head towards the dairy. 'Come on, I'll fetch you some. You can say hello to old Houdini on the way.' She stomped off up the path. They followed her, passing a field with a very high chain-link fence. On the other side of the fence stood a beautiful black goat with intelligent green eyes.

'Houdini!' said Mandy. He blinked at her and let her stroke him through the wire. 'Has he escaped recently?' Mandy asked Lydia. Houdini had been given his name because he was very good at escaping.

Lydia shook her head. 'No more escaping for

him, the old devil,' she said. 'Not with that fence. But Henry seems to be taking after him.' Henry was Houdini's young son. 'He's already got out of his field a few times.'

In the dairy, Lydia handed them three green-and-white cartons of goats' milk.

'Thanks, Lydia,' Mandy said gratefully. 'It's really kind of you.'

Lydia coughed and looked embarrassed. 'Well, you've helped me enough in the past,' she said rather gruffly. 'It's my turn to repay the favour. Just you come back whenever you want some more.'

Mandy and James put the cartons in the rucksack, said a quick hello to the other goats and then set off back down the hill to put out some goats' milk for the tabby.

When Mandy got back to Animal Ark, she put on her white coat and went through to the residential unit to see what animals were in that night. She found her mother changing a dressing on the leg of an English bull terrier. 'Hi, love,' Mrs Hope said, looking up with a smile.

Mandy hurried over. 'Do you want some help?'

'Thanks. This young chap got caught in some

barbed wire.' Mrs Hope held a new dressing firmly against the wound. 'Can you pass me a bandage?' Mandy did as her mum asked and stood ready to pass the scissors and tape. Mrs Hope worked quickly and skilfully. Mandy stroked the dog's white face. He was still sleepy from the anaesthetic. 'There, he should be good as new when that heals up.' Mrs Hope cut the end of the tape and straightened up, brushing back a long strand of red hair that had escaped from the knot at the base of her neck. 'Now, how was your day?' she asked Mandy.

As Mandy made the dog comfortable in his cage she told her mother all about the tabby cat and the notices she and James had put up.

'Hopefully *someone* will know who the cat belongs to,' Mandy said.

Mrs Hope looked up from clearing away the dressing. 'She might have been abandoned.'

Mandy nodded. 'She doesn't seem to like people very much.'

'Have you thought of a name for her?' Mrs Hope asked.

Mandy shook her head. Up to now she had just been thinking of the little tabby as 'the cat'. She ran through names in her head. Tabby . . . Tabitha . . . Socks . . . Whiskers. None of them seemed quite right. 'I'll ask James tomorrow,' she said.

Mrs Hope smiled. 'Can you finish off in here? I'll put some supper on for us. Your dad's out helping with a lambing at Fordbeck Farm.'

She left Mandy to wipe down the surfaces and settle the animals. As well as the bull terrier there was a rabbit recovering from an operation to remove a lodged fur ball and a gerbil with suspected vitamin C deficiency. As Mandy worked she thought about possible names for the cat. The bull terrier whimpered in his cage. Mandy crouched down beside him and soothed him until he went to sleep.

At last, convinced that he was happily settled, she got to her feet. 'Goodnight,' she whispered softly and quietly shut the door.

When James called for Mandy at ten to seven the next morning she had already been up for nearly an hour. She had cleaned out the cages in the residential unit and talked to the patients, all of whom were looking a bit better.

She dashed into the kitchen. Mr Hope was eating a plate of scrambled eggs. The Fordbeck Farm lambing had been followed by another call-out later in the evening and he was looking tired and bleary-eyed.

'Sit down and have some breakfast,' Mrs Hope said to Mandy.

But Mandy could hear James's bike coming up the drive. She grabbed a banana and a muesli bar from the side. 'See you later!'

'Mandy, have some breakfast!' But Mandy was out of the door, leaving her mother staring despairingly after her.

James's brown hair was tousled and he still looked half asleep. 'It's too early!' he grumbled.

Mandy grinned. 'Your jumper's on back to front.' James looked down. 'Come on!' said Mandy, leaping on her bike. 'You can change it at the Wards'.' She pedalled off down the drive.

'You know, we should think of a name for the cat,' Mandy said as James caught up.

'Tabby?' suggested James.

Mandy shook her head. 'Too boring. What about Socks?'

James shook his head. 'Sounds like a boy.' They cycled through the quiet streets exchanging names but couldn't seem to agree on anything. They passed Bill Ward's van parked by the post office in the High Street. It was seven o'clock and he was just about to start work.

'Should we knock on the door and let Mrs Ward know we're here or just put the food out?' James wondered as they arrived at the Wards' house

'Just put the food out,' decided Mandy. 'Mrs Ward might be getting ready for work and it will only make Tara bark if we knock. They know we're coming.' She left her bike against the hedge and looked over the gate. 'Look!' she breathed, grabbing James's arm as he moved to unlatch the gate.

There, lying on the grass under the cherry tree, was the tabby cat. She rolled lazily on to her back, her tail swishing through the fallen blossom. She rubbed her head and body into the ground, luxuriating in it. Clawing up a clump of blossom she pushed it up into the air. It fluttered down around her and she batted at it with her paw. Mandy realised it was the first time she had ever seen the little cat look happy.

She turned to James, her eyes shining. 'Blossom!' she whispered. 'We'll call her Blossom.'

James nodded and grinned.

Blossom eventually got up and shook herself. She trotted a little way away and sat down to groom her flanks. Mandy and James entered the garden as quietly as they could.

'Let's go straight past her,' Mandy said in a low voice. 'Don't even look at her.' They walked quietly past and dished out the food. James poured out the goats' milk into a saucer. Putting the things back in their bag, they went quietly to the porch, taking care to stay far away from the little cat.

She had stopped grooming and was watching them intently. They sat in the porch and, keeping one wary eye on them, she trotted to the food bowl. 'At least she hasn't run away,' said James. He smiled at Mandy. 'Blossom's a good name. It suits her.'

Blossom gulped down every morsel of food, lapped up the milk and then, trotting a short distance away, sat down to clean her face and whiskers. Mandy looked at the swell of the little cat's belly. 'You know I think she's expecting her kittens quite soon. She's not all that different in shape to Delilah.'

'Oh, she is,' James disagreed. 'I bet it's going to be ages yet.' But Mandy wasn't so sure.

Leaving Blossom to snooze off her breakfast, they crept out of the garden. Mandy stopped for one last look at the little cat. 'Bye, Blossom,' she said softly. The cat pricked up her ears.

Mandy stared at her. It was as though Blossom had recognised her name.

As the week passed, Blossom slowly seemed to accept Mandy and James's presence in the garden. By the end of the week, they could get to almost within a metre without her running off, but she still wouldn't let them quite near enough to touch her.

Mandy became impatient. She wanted to pick Blossom up and check her over and clean up her ear. The one consolation was that the wound seemed to be healing itself and she was sure that Blossom's ribs were sticking out a little less than they had done before. *Softly, softly,* she kept telling herself firmly. *If we rush too close too soon it could spoil everything.*

On Friday, when they stopped at the Wards' cottage after school, Blossom was nowhere to be seen but Bill Ward was standing by the shed peering inside. He looked round as they opened the gate. He beckoned them over to the shed, one finger held up to his lips, warning them to keep quiet.

Mandy and James exchanged puzzled looks but hurried over. 'Look,' said Bill. 'Look in here.' He eased the door open a little wider.

Mandy peered inside. It was dim in the shed after the brightness of outside and at first she couldn't see anything apart from tools, plant pots and gardening equipment.

Bill nodded towards one of the back corners. Mandy's eyes widened. There, sitting at the back of the shed, in an old tin bath lined with bits of newspaper, was Blossom!

'She's nesting,' Bill said. 'I saw her going in the shed once or twice yesterday. This afternoon I kept watch and there she was, nesting in that old tub. She'd dragged in an old piece of cloth I kept for wiping my hands on.' He smiled. 'I was keeping that tub to put geraniums in this summer but I guess it's got a better use now. I popped a layer of newspaper in this afternoon when she nipped out.'

Blossom stared at them. She seemed wary and cautious but it was a far cry from the blind panic she had shown when Mr Hope and Mandy had first tried to get near. 'Let's put the food down in here,' Mandy said softly.

She and James quickly sorted out the food and then slipped it halfway between the shed door and the tub. They stood back. Would Blossom come and eat it? Blossom didn't move. Mandy felt disappointed. Blossom had been letting them get that close to her in the garden.

'Better leave her to it,' said Bill. 'She'll eat when we're gone.'

'Maybe it's because she's in the shed,' James said quietly to Mandy as they slipped out the door. 'I'm sure she would have come if we'd been outside.'

Mandy looked at him gratefully. He always knew the right things to say to make her feel better. As they packed away the empty tin and dirty spoon, Mandy had a sudden thought. 'If she's nesting, then that must mean she's about to have her kittens.'

Bill Ward scratched his chin. 'Delilah's been nesting for going on two weeks now. I reckon Blossom's got a while to go yet.'

'Can we see Delilah?' James asked.

'Of course. Come on in,' Bill replied.

Mandy and James followed him into the house. Tara shot out of her basket when she saw them. Her tail thwacked against the table and the cupboards as she jumped round their legs. Mandy rubbed her ears and scratched under her chin.

'Delilah's in the sitting-room,' said Mr Ward. 'Go through if you want but shut the door so

Tara can't get in. She's a devil for jumping on the furniture.'

James held Tara back as Mandy slipped into the sitting-room and then he nimbly whizzed through the door, shutting it in Tara's disappointed face. 'Sorry, girl, but we're here to see Delilah!'

Delilah was walking around the sitting-room. Mandy reached down to stroke her but Delilah shrugged her off and continued pacing. She was breathing heavily. Her sides were moving in and out. Opening her mouth, she emitted a sharp cry.

'What's the matter with her?' James asked in alarm.

Mandy didn't reply. She was staring at the cat. A movement rippled through Delilah's body.

'James!' she gasped suddenly. 'Get Mr Ward. I think Delilah's about to have her kittens!'

Three

'You're right!' Bill Ward stared at Delilah. Another contraction rippled through the cat. 'We better see if she'll go into her box.'

'Why isn't she in there already?' asked James.

'Sometimes they like to pace,' said Bill. 'Particularly when it's their first time like Delilah here. But looking at her, I'd say she hasn't long to go now.'

He took the lid off the box and gently encouraged Delilah through the door. 'Come on then, pet. It's time you came in here.' The cat walked slowly into her box.

'Should I ring Animal Ark?' asked Mandy.

'The phone's in the kitchen,' said Bill, nodding.

Mandy dialled the number and spoke to Jean who promised to send Mr Hope along straight away. Mandy returned to the sitting-room. 'Dad will be here soon,' she said.

'Is there anything we can do?' James asked anxiously as Delilah groaned rather alarmingly.

'She's doing just fine,' Bill said calmly. 'The kittens will be some time yet. There's a box of towels ready in the kitchen. You could fetch those – and while you're in there stick the kettle on and I'll make us all a cup of tea.' James hurried off, carefully shutting the kitchen door after him so Tara couldn't come through and bother Delilah.

'Have you raised many litters of kittens?' Mandy asked Bill.

He nodded. 'When I was a lad. Delilah's my first for a while though and also my first pedigree. Still, kittening doesn't change as far as I can tell.' He looked at Delilah. 'I think she'll be another half-hour yet.' He smiled at them. 'Are you and James going to stay and watch?'

'I'd love to,' said Mandy.

'Can I ring my mum, please?' asked James, coming through with the towels. 'I should tell her where I am if we're going to be here a while.'

Bill nodded and James hurried back through to the kitchen.

They were sitting round Delilah's box when Adam Hope arrived. 'So how's the mother-to-be?' he asked, coming in and looking into the nesting box. He gently examined Delilah. 'Ah good, it all looks like it's going to plan. The first kitten's almost here. Head-first presentation. Excellent.'

Delilah sat up. Mandy could see the head emerging. She watched as a tiny white kitten eased out. Its eyes were tightly shut. Its coat was damp. Delilah turned to sever the umbilical cord that linked her to the kitten and then started to lick roughly at its face. The kitten opened its mouth and took its first breath.

'Oh!' said Mandy. 'Isn't it wonderful!' She had seen many animals being born, and had even helped in some cases, but the wonder of it never diminished for her. She looked at her father, her eyes shining.

'Nothing ever beats seeing a healthy animal born,' he said softly.

Mandy looked at Delilah cleaning her first-born. It was at times like this that Mandy knew that there was nothing in the world that she wanted more than to be a vet.

James peered rather cautiously into the

nesting box but when he saw the tiny kitten with Delilah he smiled too.

'How many more will there be?' Mandy asked her father.

'Persians don't normally have very large litters, probably only three or four,' Mr Hope replied.

They waited. Jane Ward arrived home from work and came to join them. After a bit, Delilah started to push again. Out came a second kitten, then a third and then a fourth. All white. All coming into the world easily and with no complications. After the fourth kitten had been licked clean, Delilah started to clean herself and the box.

'Well, that looks like it might be it,' said Mr Hope. 'And she didn't need us at all.' The kittens cuddled into Delilah as she settled back and started to let them feed. They lay in a row, their little tails sticking straight out behind, their heads buried in their mother's soft fur.

Mandy looked at Delilah and her four healthy kittens. She sighed happily.

'Well, we better get home,' said Mr Hope, starting to stand up. 'Do you want a lift, James? We can throw the bikes in the back.'

'Yes, please.' James and Mr Hope started to help clear away the empty mugs.

'I'll go and get Blossom's feeding bowl,' said Mandy, seizing the chance to take another quick look at the tabby cat. 'It will be easier to wash it out tonight.'

She slipped out of the back door. It was cool outside and almost dark. The light from the kitchen lit up the path to the shed. She gently opened the door and peered into the shadows. It was difficult to see. She opened the door wider to let in more light. Yes, there was Blossom, lying in the old tin bath.

Mandy stiffened. Something dark and small was lying beside her. She stared. What was it? She picked her way past plant pots and garden tools. Her foot clanged against a metal bucket and she stumbled over a bag of compost, but the tabby cat hardly even looked up. Mandy reached the tub. Her eyes widened. Lying beside Blossom was a tiny, damp kitten!

The sudden grin of delight on Mandy's face faded as quickly as it had come. Why wasn't Blossom looking after her kitten? She wasn't licking it or nursing it. Mandy swallowed hard, worry clutching her stomach. It wasn't dead, was it?

Her heart thudded. To her utter relief she saw the kitten move slightly. It was alive! The breath escaped from Mandy in a rush. She looked at Blossom and frowned. She was lying very still, not like Delilah. Delilah had been restless, moving around, changing position, seeing to the kittens.

Blossom rested her head on the newspaper. Mandy suddenly had the feeling that something was wrong, badly wrong. Blossom needed help!

Mr Hope was standing talking to the Wards in the kitchen when Mandy flung open the door. She stopped in the doorway, her blue eyes wide in her pale face. 'Quick!' she gasped. Everyone looked up in surprise.

'What's the matter?' Mr Hope asked, looking at her with concern.

'It's Blossom!' Mandy urged. 'She's having her kittens but I think something's the matter!'

Mandy turned and raced back to the shed. The others hurried after her. Bill Ward grabbed a torch from a shelf by the back door. Its powerful beam of light cut through the gloom. Blossom still lay motionless. Mr Hope took one look and then quickly started to clear a path through the boxes and pots. 'Mandy. Get my bag, please. It's in the kitchen.'

Mandy hurried into the house. Bill dug out a lamp from the shed. He hung it on a hook so that Mr Hope could see clearly. James and Jane helped to clear a path through the gardening equipment.

'What's the matter with her?' asked Mandy, as her dad leaned over and examined Blossom.

'Uterine inertia,' said Mr Hope grimly, straightening up.

James looked at Mandy for a clue as to what uterine inertia was but Mandy didn't know either. Rummaging through his bag, Mr Hope explained. 'It means that the mother cat has stopped having contractions even though there are more kittens to come out. I think there must be another kitten blocking the way. I can give her an injection to get the contractions going again but before I do that I need to find out if there is a blockage and what's causing it.'

'Should we move her inside?' asked Jane, looking worried.

Mr Hope shook his head. 'It might upset her. But if you can find any more light that would be good. And I'll need some of those towelling squares you had ready for Delilah and a hot-water bottle and a small cardboard box. I think kitten number one looks like it is going to need some help.'

Jane hurried off to the house. Mandy and James watched Blossom anxiously, counting the minutes that Jane was away.

Finally she returned, her hands full. Mr Hope picked up the kitten. 'Still alive,' he murmured, turning to Jane. 'Can I have a towel?' She handed him a towelling square and Mr Hope rubbed it firmly over the kitten. He looked at Mandy. 'Mandy, can you take over with this? I need to start on Blossom.'

'Sure,' said Mandy eagerly. She reached out and her dad placed the tiny kitten gently in her hands. 'Rub it with the towel,' he told her. 'When it's dry put it in the cardboard box. James, can you get the new box ready? It needs a layer of newspaper and then the hot-water bottle wrapped in a towel. We'll put the kittens in there.'

Mandy and James got busy with their tasks as Mr Hope started to examine Blossom. The damp kitten in the palm of Mandy's hand was tiny. She rubbed it firmly. 'Come on,' she breathed, holding it close to her face. 'You're going to be all right.'

'I was right,' Mr Hope said at last. 'There is a kitten stuck. It's in the worst position. Head turned round.'

'Can you move it?' asked Mandy, looking up anxiously from rubbing the kitten.

Mr Hope's face was serious. 'I'll try. It's really our only hope. Blossom's so weak and undernourished I doubt she could survive a Caesarean operation.'

'What about the kitten inside?' James asked, putting the cardboard box next to Mandy. 'Will it be OK?'

'It depends how long it's been there,' said Mr Hope. 'There's a limit to the length of time a kitten can survive in the birth canal like that. We might well be too late.'

Mandy's heart sank. She placed the first tiny kitten in the box and covered it up. It was dry now and she knew it needed the heat from the hot-water bottle. She watched anxiously as her dad tried to help Blossom, his face set with concentration.

Time dragged by. Mandy felt close to tears. *Poor, poor little Blossom.* Mr Hope was a brilliant vet, one of the best, but Mandy knew the harsh realities of a vet's life. Sometimes, being brilliant wasn't enough.

'I can't get it round,' Mr Hope muttered.

Fingers of despair curled round Mandy's heart. Bill Ward looked on, a deeply worried look on his normally cheerful face.

Mr Hope shook his head. 'No, it's not coming . . . yes!' he suddenly exclaimed. 'It's there!'

He straightened up. 'It's turned.'

'Oh, Dad!' gasped Mandy. 'Well done.'

Mr Hope reached for a syringe in his bag and injected Blossom. 'Now the contractions should start again.'

Mandy leaned forward. 'Is the kitten still alive?'

Mr Hope shrugged. 'We'll just have to wait and see.'

The injection started to work its magic. Gradually contractions started to ripple through Blossom's sides. Mandy crossed her fingers. The second kitten started to appear. It slithered out, head first, on to the paper.

Everyone held their breath as Blossom started to nose at it and lick it. She cleaned its face and nostrils but the kitten lay still.

'Too late,' muttered Bill, shaking his head.

Mandy's mouth went dry. She looked at her father. He was leaning forward with a speculative look in his eyes, peering at the ginger kitten. Hope flickered through her. 'Dad?' Mandy faltered. *Had he seen something?* And then she saw it too. The kitten moved. Everyone gasped. 'It's alive!' Mandy cried.

Blossom started to clean the kitten vigorously. James pushed a relieved hand through his tousled hair. Bill put his arm round Jane's shoulders and hugged her. 'Not too late after all,' said Mr Hope smiling at Mandy.

Mandy's legs suddenly felt wobbly. The kitten had survived. Both mother and baby had been saved. She watched in delight as Blossom gave birth to one more kitten and immediately began licking it. 'I think that's her lot,' said Mr Hope, watching Blossom finish cleaning the kitten and then herself. The two little kittens beside her pushed through her fur towards her teats. Mr Hope picked them out one by one and looked under their tails. 'It's always easiest to sex them when they are newborn,' he explained to the watchers. 'The ginger one's obviously a boy. The tabby's a girl.'

Mandy picked up the cardboard box. 'What about this one?'

Mr Hope took the tabby-and-white kitten out of the cardboard box and examined her quickly. 'Another girl,' he said with a smile, placing her carefully next to her litter mates. Blossom settled back happily to let her three babies feed.

As everyone left the shed, Mandy lingered for one moment more to look at the sleeping kittens. A warm glow of happiness spread through her.

Two mothers. Seven kittens.

What an evening!

Four

The next morning, Mandy and James bumped along the track to High Cross Farm. The sun was shining brightly but the wind on the hillside was cold and Mandy was glad of her gloves. She inhaled deeply. She loved this time of year, everything growing, the fields clothed in fresh, green grass, young animals being born.

She thought about the kittens at the Wards' house. She and James had called in there first thing but the kittens and the two mother cats had all been asleep so they had decided to go up to High Cross Farm to fetch some more milk.

Leaving their bikes by the farmhouse they went in search of Lydia. 'Let's try the barn,' said James, heading over to a long, low building. 'She's probably in there.'

They unlatched the heavy barn door and found Lydia mucking out the goats' pens inside. 'Morning,' she said cheerily. 'Come for some more milk?'

'If you don't mind,' said Mandy.

Lydia looked surprised. 'Of course not. I said to come any time. You should know by now that I always mean what I say. Now, you might as well make yourself useful. I could do with some fresh straw over here.'

Mandy grinned. Lydia could be a bit brusque sometimes but her heart was in the right place. Carrying the golden straw over, Mandy told Lydia all about the kittens. James stopped to stroke a small black goat in a pen near the door.

'Watch him!' Lydia warned. 'He'll try to eat your jumper.' James jumped back just in time. Lydia chuckled. 'Henry will eat anything, the little devil.' She nodded at James. 'Can you pass me that brush?'

Mandy and James busied themselves. The goats pushed against the bars of their pens, seeking attention.

There was the sudden clunk of a metal bolt drawing back. Mandy, James and Lydia swung round. Henry was pulling back the bolt on his pen with his strong teeth.

'Quick! Stop him!' Mandy gasped to James as Henry pushed the pen door open with his nose.

James leaped towards the little black goat. With an excited bleat, Henry shot out of his pen and took off down the passageway.

'The main door's open!' James exclaimed. 'I didn't lock it behind me!'

'Oh no!' groaned Lydia.

The three of them started to run after Henry but it was too late. The little goat had reached the main door. He butted it with his head. It creaked open and he leaped joyfully outside.

Mandy, James and Lydia charged after him. His head held high, Henry trotted over to Houdini's field. He began to graze on the tufts of grass growing outside the enclosure.

'Come on, Henry. Come here,' coaxed Lydia, getting a carrot out of her pocket. Henry lifted his head but wasn't sufficiently tempted to give up his freedom for one measly carrot. He took a step farther away from them towards the drive.

Lydia looked worried. 'He mustn't go down the drive. He'd be over the gate in a second and then we'd never catch him.'

'I'll cut him off,' said James quickly. 'If I go

across the grass, I can get to the gate and block him if he reaches it.' He set off across the field. Mandy and Lydia edged towards Henry. Lydia waved the carrot again. Henry's nose twitched.

'Quietly now,' Lydia murmured to her, her eyes never leaving the goat. 'While he's looking at me see if you can get round in front of him and shoo him towards me, away from the drive.'

Mandy started to sidle round the little goat. His ears twitched back and forth. She got a little bit closer and, all of a sudden, tripped over a cobblestone and crashed to the ground. Henry leaped up into the air and, turning on the spot, set off at a joyful canter down the drive.

Mandy scrambled to her feet and raced after him, her heart pounding. To her relief she saw James running up the drive towards the goat, waving his arms. Henry snorted in surprise and then cantered back up the drive. He swerved past Mandy's outstretched arms.

'He's heading for the top field,' gasped Mandy. 'Come on, James!'

They raced up the drive. Suddenly, just as Henry reached the track that led towards the fields, there was a loud rattling. Henry stopped dead and bleated.

'Henry!' Lydia was standing by an outbuilding

shaking the door vigorously. 'Supper!'

Henry pricked his ears and set off towards Lydia at a fast trot. Lydia opened the door and, as he pushed inside, she caught him firmly by his collar. 'Got him!' she cried triumphantly.

Mandy and James looked at each other in amazement and hurried over. 'What happened?' Mandy asked astonished. 'How did you get him to come?'

Lydia smiled and gave Henry his carrot. 'This is my new feed-room. All the goats know that they get fed when they hear the door rattle. Henry's just too greedy to resist.'

Mandy and James followed her as she led the little goat firmly back to the barn. The other goats were peering out of their pens, their ears pricked in excitement. 'I'll have to give them a bit of food or they'll never settle down,' said Lydia, putting Henry in his pen. 'No more escaping for you,' she told him firmly, as she fixed the safety clip securely on to the bolt on Henry's door.

'I'm sorry I left the barn door open,' said James, rather shamefaced.

'All's well that ends well, as my father used to say,' said Lydia. 'I should have had the safety clip on, but when I'm mucking out I often leave it off until I've finished going in and out.'

Mandy and James helped her scoop out some oats and barley into buckets in the new feed-room. The floor was flagged with large, grey stones. Around the walls stood strong metal feed-bins, buckets, bags of old vegetables and some huge, unopened sacks of oats and barley. Previously Lydia had just kept the food in bins in the barn.

'I was offered a large amount of food at a cheap price,' Lydia explained. 'And I didn't have enough room in the barn so I decided that I would use this place.' She threw the scoop back into the bin of barley. 'The only trouble is, I hadn't bargained on the rats and mice.' She nodded towards the feed-bags. Several had holes nibbled in them and feed was spilling out on to the floor. 'They're going to eat more of it than the goats if I don't do something soon.'

'Can't you get some more feed-bins?' said James.

'They're very expensive,' Lydia said. 'And anyway it's not just in here that the mice are causing a problem. They're in the house and in the hayloft too. They seem to be taking over the place. I've put down traps, but it doesn't seem to be stopping them.'

'You should get a cat,' said Mandy.

Lydia shook her head. 'Me? No, I don't like cats. Cold, unfriendly creatures. Definitely not.' She picked up the feed buckets. 'Let's feed these goats and then we can get you that milk.'

'Do you think Blossom will be scared of us today?' Mandy asked James as they walked through the Wards' garden gate. It was a question that had been preying on her mind. The night before the little cat had been too ill to worry about their presence but what would she be like now that she had recovered?

'There's only one way to find out,' said James, pushing his glasses firmly on to his nose. They opened the shed door. Blossom was sitting up in the tub. She stared at them with her wide green eyes.

'Do you want some breakfast?' Mandy asked. She filled a bowl with the fresh goats' milk and placed it quietly by Blossom's tub. To her delight, the little cat jumped out of the tub, stalked over and started to lap. Mandy cautiously knelt down beside her. Blossom continued to drink. Mandy stroked her. The tabby glanced up but her eyes had lost their fear. *She knows we helped her,* Mandy thought, a warm glow of happiness spreading through her.

'Look at the kittens,' James said.

Mandy straightened up and looked in the tub. The three kittens were snuggled in a heap, their eyes tightly shut. Mandy knew that all kittens were born deaf and blind. She longed to touch them but thought Blossom might not like it. 'I can't wait till they open their eyes,' she said.

James nodded. 'It happens when they are about five days old, doesn't it?' he said.

'Well, sometime between three and ten days old,' said Mandy. 'We'll need to think of names for them. They should be called something that goes with Blossom.'

James thought for a moment. 'You can get different types of blossom. There's cherry blossom, like on the tree outside. We could call one little girl kitten Cherry. And what about Peaches for the other one?'

'Cherry and Peaches,' said Mandy, thinking about it. 'OK, they're good names.' She pointed to the tabby one who looked just like Blossom. 'That one can be Cherry and the other one can be Peaches.' She frowned and looked at the ginger tom kitten. 'But what about him?'

James scratched his nose. 'Apple? Apricot? Pear?'

'You can't call a cat any of those!' said Mandy, grinning.

They thought for a moment longer.

'What about William?' James suggested.

'But it's not a blossom,' objected Mandy.

'It is,' said James triumphantly. 'You can get William pears, and William pear trees would have blossom.'

'Brilliant!' Mandy agreed, smiling. She looked at the little ginger kitten. 'William it is then.'

Leaving Blossom to eat her breakfast, they knocked on the back door. Jane Ward answered. They told her about naming Blossom's kittens. 'We've thought of names for Delilah's too,' she told them. 'Do you want to come in and see them?'

'Where's Tara?' asked James, looking round as they walked through to the sitting-room.

'Out with Bill on his rounds,' Jane explained. 'She keeps trying to get into the sitting-room to see what's in there. But we're going to leave it a few days before introducing her to the kittens.'

'What names have you chosen?' Mandy asked eagerly as she and James followed Mrs Ward through to the sitting-room.

'The two little girls are going to be Desdemona and Daisy and the two little boys Daniel and Dylan.'

Mandy and James knelt by the nesting box. Delilah was awake and the kittens were feeding. The four little white bodies were all in a line.

'They look identical,' said James. 'How are you going to tell which is which?'

Jane smiled and pointed to four bottles of nail varnish on the mantelpiece. Each bottle was a different colour and each bottle had a kitten name stuck to it. 'I've put a dab of a different colour on each kitten,' she told them. 'Just on one of their front claws. All I have to do is look at the colour and then I know which kitten it is.'

'That's clever,' said Mandy. She peered closer. 'So which *is* which?'

'The bright pink is Desdemona, the pale pink is Daisy, the red is Dylan and the plum colour is Daniel.'

The kittens squirmed and pushed to get at Delilah's teats. Mandy noticed one kitten seemed particularly good at edging the others out of the way. He scrabbled and shoved and climbed over his brother and sisters. Mandy checked the colour of the nail varnish. It was red. She checked the labels on the bottles. That meant he must be Dylan. She smiled. Using the nail varnish was a really good way of telling the kittens apart.

'They don't do very much at the moment, do they?' said James, as one by one the kittens stopped drinking and fell asleep where they lay.

Jane shook her head. 'They will when they start opening their eyes.'

Mandy frowned. 'Delilah has amber eyes but her mother, Duchess, has blue. Do you know what colour eyes the kittens will have?'

'We hope amber,' said Jane. 'White cats with blue eyes are often deaf. Duchess isn't, but she's quite rare. All kittens have blue eyes to start with but they start changing once the kittens reach three months old.' She smiled rather anxiously at Mandy and James. 'Fingers crossed, they'll all be fine.'

Mandy looked down at the sleeping kittens, all snuggled into one big heap. They looked so perfect. She couldn't bear the thought that one or more of them might be deaf. Surely they would all be all right?

Mandy and James visited the two sets of kittens each day, calling in morning and evening when they stopped off to feed Blossom. 'William's going exploring again,' Mandy pointed out as she and James crouched by Blossom's tub after school on Tuesday.

Cherry and Peaches were lying contentedly beside their mother but William, the little ginger kitten, was slowly pushing himself across the bottom of the tub. He couldn't walk yet so he was sliding on his tummy, using his back legs. He reached the side of the tub and stopped.

James laughed. 'I bet he's going to be adventurous when he gets older.'

'Cherry's not,' Mandy smiled, glancing at the little tabby kitten who was snuggled as far as she could be into Blossom's soft fur. 'She never leaves Blossom's side.' She reached in and gently picked up Peaches. Blossom hardly flickered an eyelid. She was used to Mandy and James handling her precious kittens now. 'What about you, Peaches?' Mandy said, feeling the tiny pin-pricks of Peaches' claws. 'What are you going to be like?'

The little tabby-and-white kitten lifted her head and blinked at her. 'James!' Mandy gasped, almost dropping the kitten in amazement. 'Look! She's opening her eyes!'

They gazed speechlessly at Peaches. She blinked again and this time kept her eyes open. She looked around. Her eyes were a deep, dark blue. Opening her mouth, she miaowed.

Mandy and James laughed. Carefully Mandy put her back into the tub. 'That must mean that the others are about to open their eyes too,' she said. They picked up William and Cherry but their eyes were still closed.

'Maybe they will have opened them by tomorrow,' said James, hopefully.

James was right. When they stopped off to feed Blossom the next morning they found William and Cherry blinking in the shaft of sunlight that was shining in through the dusty shed window. 'They won't be able to see very much to start with,' said Mandy. 'But their eyesight will gradually get stronger.' She smiled. 'Don't they look adorable?'

Just then, there was the sound of feet coming along the path and Jane Ward poked her head round the shed door. She was wearing her dressing-gown and slippers. 'I thought I heard you come in through the gate.' She looked pleased and excited. 'Come and see Delilah's kittens. They've just opened their eyes!'

Mandy and James peered into Delilah's nesting box. Desdemona, Daisy, Dylan and Daniel all blinked up, their large eyes looking extra-blue against the white of their fur.

'It's amazing how Delilah's and Blossom's

litters have opened their eyes at exactly the same time,' said Mandy.

Jane Ward nodded. 'And now they've opened their eyes the fun and games will *really* start. They'll be trying to walk in another week.'

'Seven kittens!' said James. 'Just think what mischief they could get up to!'

It took a while for the kittens to get used to walking, but by the time they were almost three weeks old, they were all toddling around on their short, unsteady legs. Most of the time they moved round with their large heads close to the ground, stopping occasionally to roll over and play. Mandy felt that she could quite happily have sat and watched them all day.

'Each day they do something different,' she told her mum as she helped clean up after Thursday evening surgery. 'They've started trying to bite each other now. Dylan was the first to start and now they're all doing it.' She squeezed out the mop she was using and looked across at her mother. 'Mum . . .' She stopped.

Mrs Hope looked up from sorting her paperwork. 'Is something on your mind?' she asked, studying Mandy's face,

Mandy nodded. Ever since Mrs Ward had

mentioned the link between blue eyes and deafness she had been thinking about Delilah's kittens. 'What would happen if one of Delilah's kittens was deaf?'

Mrs Hope rubbed her forehead. 'Well, I expect Bill and Jane Ward would try to find a good home for it but it would be difficult.' She saw Mandy's worried face. 'How old are the kittens now?'

'Three weeks old tomorrow.'

Mrs Hope smiled. 'And adorable?'

'Completely,' said Mandy.

Mrs Hope tidied up her paperwork. 'If they're three weeks then they should be about old enough to have their hearing tested.'

Mandy's eyes lit up. 'Is it difficult to test them? Could I do it?'

Mrs Hope shook her head. 'Oh no, you *definitely* need a trained vet.' She looked thoughtful. 'If Jane doesn't mind, I could pop along after morning surgery on Saturday. Maybe I'll give her a ring and see what she thinks.'

'Could you?' asked Mandy eagerly. If there was a way of telling whether any of the kittens were deaf then she wanted to know. But what would happen if one of the kittens *was* deaf? What would the Wards do then?

* * *

The four white kittens walked unsteadily around their run, stopping occasionally to climb over one another. Dylan pawed at Daisy's face and knocked her over. She rolled on her back and he tried to bite her. Daniel watched from a safe distance. He was the most timid of Delilah's four kittens.

It was Saturday afternoon, Jane Ward had gladly accepted Mrs Hope's offer to come and test the kittens' hearing. Mrs Hope took the kittens out of the box one at a time and examined them thoroughly. Delilah sat on the carpet and watched. 'Very healthy,' Mrs Hope pronounced.

'But are they deaf?' Mandy asked anxiously. 'How will you tell?'

Mrs Hope smiled. 'Ah yes. Now this is a really complicated test. Are you watching carefully?'

Mandy nodded. Mrs Hope put Dylan down on a towel on the floor. He took a few wobbly steps. Mandy waited eagerly. She wondered what her mother was going to do.

All of a sudden, Mrs Hope clapped her hands loudly a little way behind the kitten. Dylan started and looked round curiously.

'There we are,' said Mrs Hope with a smile at Mandy. 'Not deaf.'

Mandy stared. 'Is that all you do? But you said it was really complicated!'

Mrs Hope's green eyes twinkled. 'I just wanted an excuse to see the kittens.'

'Mum!'

Mrs Hope picked Dylan up and cuddled him. 'I love kittens.' She turned to Jane. 'Don't worry, I won't be charging you for this visit.' Putting Dylan in the box she took Daniel out. 'You have to be sure that the kitten can't see you doing it,' she explained to Mandy. 'And you mustn't clap too close or drop something on the floor to make a noise because then the kitten might feel the vibrations and turn round.'

Mandy watched as her mother tested Daniel. He too was given the all clear although he almost fell over in fright at the loud sound. 'Scaredy-cat!' said Mandy, laughing and putting him back in the safety of the box. She turned to her mum. 'Can I try with the next one?' When Mrs Hope nodded, Mandy carefully picked Desdemona out of the box and put her down on the floor. When Desdemona's back was turned she clapped her hands. Desdemona jumped. Mandy smiled in relief. 'She's all right.'

Daisy was the last kitten to be tested. Mandy held her breath and clapped. To her delight,

Daisy jumped and looked round as well. Seeing Mandy she came towards her, stopping and putting her tiny paws on Mandy's knee. Daisy miaowed loudly, looking up with her dark blue eyes.

'I think she wants to be picked up,' said Jane Ward with a laugh. 'She seems to love being cuddled. She's always the first to come over when you look in the pen.' Mandy scooped the little kitten up and cradled her in the crook of her arm.

Jane Ward and Mrs Hope stood up. 'I think you've got a wonderful, healthy litter there,' said Mrs Hope. 'It's a pleasure to see kittens so well looked after.'

'It's all really down to Delilah,' said Jane. 'She does most of the looking after, the cleaning and feeding.'

'Where is Delilah?' asked Mandy, putting Daisy back into the box and looking round.

Delilah was no longer sitting in the sitting-room. 'She's probably gone for a little wander,' said Jane. 'She's just started leaving the kittens for longer periods of time. I'm trying to keep an eye on her though. I don't really think she's got her road sense back yet.'

Mandy looked out of the window. Delilah was

walking across the grass of the front garden. As Mandy watched she jumped on to the gatepost. 'Mrs Ward,' said Mandy, anxiously. 'Delilah's got out.'

Jane looked out of the window and sighed. 'I'd better go and get her.' She headed for the back door.

'And I'd better be getting back home,' said Mrs Hope, picking up her bag and following Mrs Ward out. 'I take it you're going to stay here for a bit longer, Mandy?'

Before Mandy had a chance to reply there was a screaming of brakes from the road.

Mandy looked back at the gatepost. 'Delilah!' she gasped. Delilah was no longer there. Mandy shot a horrified look at her mother. They dashed down the garden path towards the road.

Five

'Oh no!' cried Jane Ward, her hands flying to her mouth. Delilah was lying completely still in the middle of the road.

'Quick, Mandy!' said Mrs Hope. They ran over and knelt beside the motionless cat. A sob caught in Mandy's throat. Delilah's eyes were closed. Bright red blood was spurting out of a wound on her leg.

'She's still breathing,' said Mrs Hope. She looked up quickly. 'We need to get her off this road. Can you find me something flat to move her on, Mandy? We need to keep her as still as possible.'

'There's a piece of wood in the shed,' said Mandy.

'Get that, please. Jane, can you keep an eye on the road and check nothing else comes?' Not waiting for an answer, Mrs Hope bent her head and gently started to examine Delilah.

Mandy ran to the shed. Her heart was racing, her breath was coming in short gasps. Hot tears burned against the back of her eyes but she knew she had to keep a clear head if she was going to help her mother try to save Delilah.

Together, they eased Delilah's still, white body on to the plank of wood and lifted her to the side of the road. Jane hovered anxiously behind them. 'I can't believe the driver didn't even stop,' she kept repeating dazedly.

Mrs Hope opened her bag and knelt beside Delilah. 'She's in shock,' she said to Mandy. 'We need to stop this bleeding and get her to Animal Ark immediately.' She pressed firmly on the blood vessel to stem the furious flow. 'Can you pass me a thick wad of dressing and a bandage from my bag?'

Mandy already had the bag open. She held Delilah's leg steady while her mother applied a pressure bandage. Without needing to be asked she passed over the tape and the scissors. Her heart was pounding but her mind was clear as she concentrated on assisting her mother as efficiently as possible. Every second was vital. 'That will do,' Mrs Hope said, throwing everything into her bag and jumping swiftly to her feet. 'Let's get her into the Land-rover.'

They lifted Delilah carefully into the back. 'Will you be able to save her?' Jane Ward whispered. Mandy turned and saw the anguish on her face.

Mrs Hope reached to shut the back of the Land-rover. 'I can't tell, Jane.' Her green eyes were warm with sympathy. 'But I promise we'll do all we can. Can you follow us to the surgery? We'll be able to find out more there.'

It was silent and tense in the Land-rover on the way back to Animal Ark. Mandy felt sick to her stomach. 'Mandy, love,' Mrs Hope said, glancing over, 'can you ring the surgery and let them know we're coming in, please.'

Mandy punched the numbers into the mobile phone.

'Animal Ark.' It was her dad. Hearing his deep, warm voice Mandy almost gave way to the tears that were burning behind her eyes, but she forced herself to speak calmly. She explained quickly about Delilah. 'We're coming straight in,' she told him. 'Mrs Ward's following us.'

'I'll get the operating room ready,' Mr Hope said quickly. 'Try not to worry. You'll be here soon.'

But would 'soon' be too late? thought Mandy. She put the phone down and turned to look at Delilah. Her heart sank. The cat was lying motionless in the back. *Oh please,* she thought, a lump of tears swelling in her throat. *Please let us be in time.*

Mr Hope and Simon were waiting at Animal Ark. They hurried out as the Land-rover stopped, and lifted Delilah out of the back. Mrs Hope grabbed her white coat from the office and followed them into the operating room.

'Can I come in?' asked Mandy, running after her.

Mrs Hope shook her head. 'Not this time, Mandy,' she said gently.

Mandy stared as the door of the operating room shut. She was normally allowed in to watch operations. Why not this one? The only answer possible thumped in her heart. Her mum thought Delilah wasn't going to survive.

The waiting-room door flew open and Jane Ward came hurrying in. 'Where is she?' she asked wildly.

'In the operating room,' said Mandy.

Jane sank down on to one of the seats and buried her head in her hands. Mandy could see her shoulders shaking. She sat down next to her. 'Mum and Dad will do everything they can,' she said, trying to sound as confident as possible. Jane didn't reply.

Bill Ward arrived. With tears running down her cheeks, Jane told him what had happened. He sat down beside her and took her hand.

The minutes ticked by slowly.

Half an hour later, the door opened. All three of them jumped to their feet as Mrs Hope came out. She was pushing the hair back from her face. Mandy searched her eyes. What news did she have?

'What's happened?' asked Jane. 'Is she . . . ? Is she . . . ?'

'Delilah's badly injured but we think she's going to survive,' said Mrs Hope.

Relief rushed through Mandy, her legs went wobbly and she suddenly had to sit down again. Bill hugged Jane.

'The X-rays show that Delilah has a slight fracture of her pelvis and two broken ribs,' Mrs Hope continued. 'But luckily there appears to be no internal haemorrhaging. The next twenty-four hours will be critical but at the moment the signs are good.'

'Can we see her?' asked Jane.

'Of course, come through.'

Mr Hope and Simon were putting things away. They left the operating room so Mrs Hope could talk to the Wards. Mandy went straight to where Delilah was lying on the operating table. A new bandage had replaced the old one on the cat's leg. Her eyes were closed but her breathing had slowed down.

Bill came and stood behind Mandy. 'Poor lass,' he said, shaking his head.

Mrs Hope got out a set of X-rays and displayed them against a light-box. She pointed out the fracture in Delilah's pelvis. 'Luckily, Delilah has escaped with only a slight fracture. Serious fractures in this area nearly always result in the cat needing to be put to sleep.'

'Do you have to operate or anything to mend it?' asked Jane.

Mrs Hope shook her head. 'Hopefully this and the broken ribs will self-heal,' she said. 'It may take up to two months and she will have to be cage-rested for at least part of the time in order to avoid any aggravation of her injuries.'

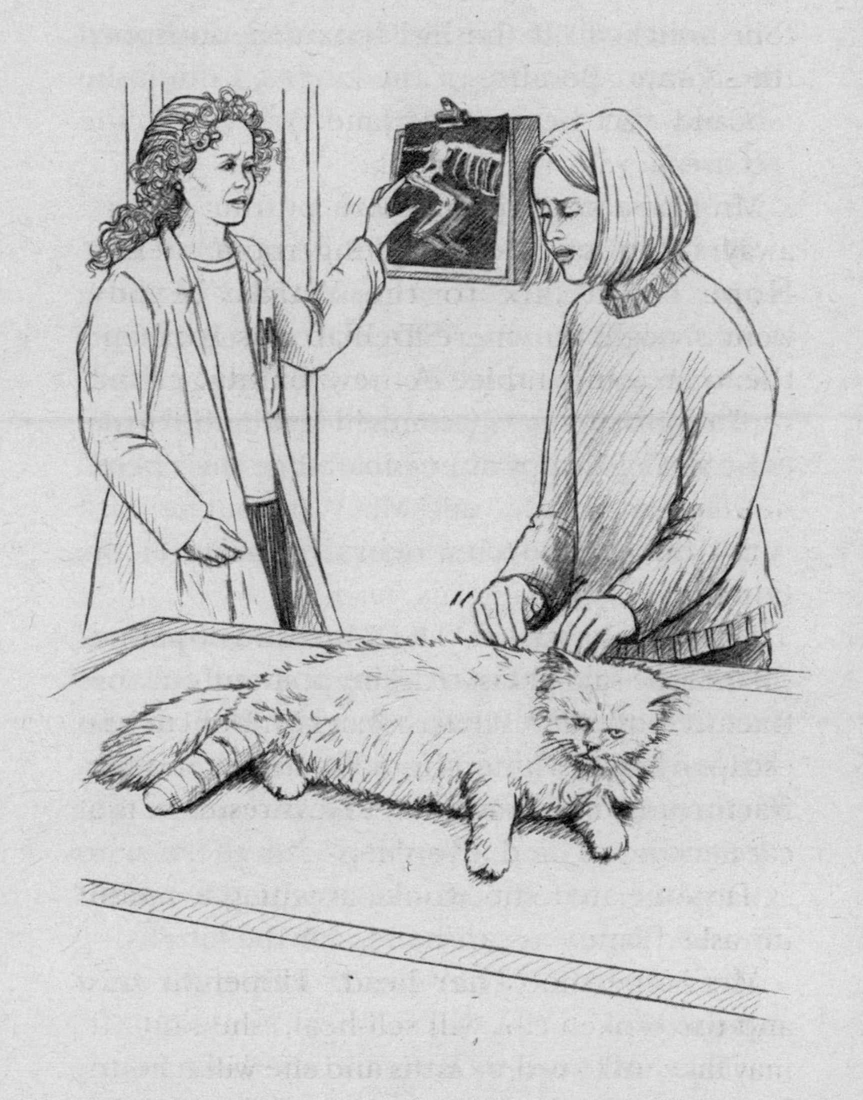

She switched off the light-box and unclipped the X-rays. 'Because of the kittens, I think she should stay here at Animal Ark while she recovers.'

'For how long?' Jane asked.

Mrs Hope stroked Delilah's head. 'We'll have to see how her recovery goes. It may be three weeks, possibly more.' She looked sympathetic. 'You can come and see her as often as you want.'

'I'll look after her,' promised Mandy. 'I'll make sure she's as happy as possible while she's here.'

'Thanks, Mandy,' said Mrs Ward but her face was troubled. 'So what does this mean for the kittens?'

There was a pause. 'There are three options,' Mrs Hope said at last, tucking a strand of loose hair behind her left ear. 'One, to find a cat who has lost her own kittens to act as a foster mother. Unfortunately I don't know of any such cats at the moment and even if I did there's no guarantee that she would accept the kittens anyway. Two, you can hand-rear the kittens.'

Jane nodded. 'That's what I thought we'd have to do.'

'They will need to be fed every three hours, starting at about six in the morning and going through till midnight. It will be an almost full-time job for the next three or four weeks until they are weaned. Luckily, they are old enough to go through the night without being fed.'

Jane started to look worried. 'But I'm at work all day and Bill's not in till gone half past one.' She frowned. 'We could maybe ask someone to help us.'

Bill scratched his chin. 'It's asking a lot of anyone. Who do we know who could spare the time?'

Mandy looked at her mum. 'Couldn't the kittens come and stay here?'

Mrs Hope shook her head. 'With the lambing season coming to its peak we're just too busy, Mandy. Simon will have enough to do coping with the patients here while Dad and I are out on call.'

'You said there was a third option?' said Bill.

Mrs Hope sighed. 'The third option is to put them to sleep.'

'No!' gasped Mandy, horrified.

Jane immediately started shaking her head. 'Oh no, no, I couldn't.'

'Mum, that's...'

Mrs Hope shot Mandy a very stern look and Mandy bit back her words. She knew that, no matter how hard it was, she must never interfere when her mother was giving a professional opinion. Deep down, her mum would no sooner want to have the kittens put down than Mandy herself, but, as a vet, it was her duty to give her clients what she felt to be the most honest and practical advice possible.

Mrs Hope's eyes searched the Wards' faces.

'Oh, what are we going to do?' Jane said, despairingly.

'Mandy, would you go and get a cage ready for Delilah in the residential unit, please,' Mrs Hope said. Mandy stared desperately at her. She couldn't bear the thought that the kittens' fate would be decided without her in the room.

'Mandy,' Mrs Hope insisted, her eyes demanding obedience.

Not trusting herself to speak, Mandy turned and walked out of the room.

As soon as she shut the door a huge sob burst from her. She ran into the residential unit and collapsed in a heap by the door, giving way to a flood of tears. Surely the Wards wouldn't put Delilah's kittens down? How could they? If only there was something she could do. She thought of how the kittens had been earlier that day, play-fighting and toddling round their box. But it was the Wards' decision. Burying her head in her hands, she cried noisily.

The door opened. 'Mandy?' It was Mr Hope. His face creased in concern. 'Mandy, whatever's the matter?'

'Oh, Dad!' sobbed Mandy, hardly able to get the words out. 'It's the kittens!'

Mr Hope hurried over and, kneeling down beside her, put his arm round her slim shoulders. 'Come on, tell me all about it.'

Her body shaking with great gasping sobs, Mandy explained. 'There's no one to look after them,' she said. 'The Wards are out at work and they don't know anyone who can help. They're going to be put down! Oh, Dad, I can't bear it!'

'Hang on, hang on,' said Mr Hope, his kind eyes probing her face. 'Aren't you and James on half-term next week?'

Mandy nodded as she sobbed against his shoulder. Suddenly the significance of his words hit her. She sat bolt upright and stared at him. 'You mean James and I could help look after them?'

Mr Hope nodded.

'But we're only on holiday for a week,' Mandy said despairingly. 'And the kittens will need hand-rearing for at least three or four more weeks.'

'But a week gives you time to try and find someone else who can take over when you go back to school,' pointed out Mr Hope. 'Isn't it worth a try?' He squeezed her shoulder. 'Look, why don't you go and ask Mum?'

Mandy stared at him, the tears drying on her face. 'Do you think she'll say yes?'

'What do you think?' said Mr Hope.

Mrs Hope and the Wards looked up in surprise as Mandy burst into the operating room. 'We can help you!' she cried. 'James and I! We're on half-term next week. We can look after the kittens while you're at work.' She gabbled the words out as fast as she could.

For a moment they all just stared.

'But, Mandy, love, what will happen when you and James go back to school at the end of the week?' asked Mrs Hope, the quickest to recover.

'We'll think of *something*,' said Mandy desperately. 'We can ask around. We'll find someone who can help.' She looked round at them all. Her blue eyes started to plead. 'At least give us a chance to try.'

Mrs Hope turned to the Wards. 'Well, it's up to you.'

Jane Ward's face broke into a smile. 'We'd really love your help, Mandy, wouldn't we, Bill?'

'If you're sure you've got the time?' he said to Mandy.

Mandy nodded eagerly. She looked at her mother and saw the relief in her eyes. 'Well, it certainly does seem like a good solution,' Mrs Hope said. She shot Mandy a glance. 'It will be hard work though. Sometimes kittens don't like formula milk.'

'I don't care how hard I've got to work,' said Mandy, her own eyes shining with determination. 'I just want Delilah's kittens to have a chance.'

Six

'Have you got everything we need?' James called as they cycled along. As soon as Mandy had rung him to tell him about how they were going to spend their half-term holiday he had come straight round.

Mandy nodded. They were on their way to give the kittens their first bottle feed. Her rucksack was heavy with feeding bottles, bags of formula milk and other equipment that her mother had thought they might need.

Jane Ward was waiting for them in the kitchen. She had emptied a shelf in one of the cupboards for them. 'You can leave everything in here. Out, Tara!' she said as the dog tried to investigate the bags of formula milk. 'I think you'd better go outside.' Taking Tara firmly by the collar she steered her out into the back garden.

Mandy opened a bag of formula milk. 'Have you got a fork we could use, Mrs Ward?'

Jane handed her a fork and watched as James measured out the fine, creamy-coloured powder with a tiny scoop and then Mandy used the fork to mix the powder with some water. 'You look like you've done this before,' she said.

Mandy grinned. 'We have. Lots of times.'

'Kittens, puppies, lambs, goats,' James put in. 'We've helped bottle-feed all sorts of young animals.'

Jane smiled and went through to fetch the first two kittens. 'So, I'm getting a lesson from the experts then.'

After ten minutes of trying to get Dylan and Daniel to accept some milk, Mandy and James were feeling far from expert. The milk was on their hands, on their jeans and on the kittens' fur, but none of it had seemed to go into a kitten's mouth. 'I see what Mum meant about kittens sometimes being awkward!' said Mandy, struggling to hold Dylan. 'Come on, you *want* this milk.'

But Dylan was adamant that he didn't. He shut his mouth tight and moved his head around.

On the other side of the table, James was faring equally badly with Daniel. 'This is a nightmare!' he said to Mandy as Daniel almost managed to throw himself on to the floor.

'They don't seem to want to drink anything,' said Jane, looking worried.

The two little kittens mewed pitifully.

Blossom poked her head round the kitchen door. She stalked over to James and stared at him.

'It's all right, Blossom,' James said. 'We're not hurting them.'

'We're not managing to feed them much either,' said Mandy.

'Should I hold one?' Jane offered. She took Daniel and held him firmly. It was a bit easier with two people, one to hold and one to feed and at last both kittens had taken some milk. Mandy cleaned them up with a warm, damp cloth and then put them back in the box.

'Time for the next two,' she said to James. Looking less than enthusiastic, James picked up Daisy. 'I hope she's not as bad as Daniel,' he said.

If anything, Daisy was even worse. By the time Daisy and Desdemona were fed both Mandy and James were once again covered in spilled milk. 'Thank goodness that's over!' said James, putting Daisy down in the box.

Mandy watched the kittens. Normally, after eating, they would fall asleep curled up by Delilah but now they wandered round, opening their mouths wide and mewing. She sighed. They were missing their mum.

'If only there was something we could do to make them happier,' she said. But she knew the only thing that would make a difference would be Delilah.

James and Mandy agreed to meet up the following morning at eight o'clock to feed Blossom and to help the Wards with the kittens' nine o'clock feed. As soon as Mandy got back to Animal Ark, she went straight to the residential unit to check on Delilah. It was Simon's afternoon off but he had offered to stay to keep an eye on Delilah's recovery. He was sitting next to her cage, reading a book about badgers. 'Hi there,' he said as Mandy came in.

'How is she?' Mandy asked eagerly, looking

in the cage. Delilah was lying flat out on a fleecy white blanket. Her breathing was slow and deep. Her eyes were closed.

'She's coming round slowly,' Simon said, standing up and looking over Mandy's shoulder. 'But she'll be kept sedated so she doesn't try to move too much at the moment. How were the kittens?'

Mandy sighed. 'Oh, Simon, it's so difficult to get them to feed.' She looked at him hopefully; he could normally be relied on when it came to looking after animals. 'Any ideas?'

But this time even Simon couldn't help her. 'Sorry,' he said, shrugging sympathetically. 'But I don't think there are any magic solutions to bottle-feeding kittens. Just keep trying. I've got a book on cats with a good chapter on bringing up orphan kittens, if you want to read it.'

'Yes, please!' said Mandy. 'I think I need all the advice I can get.'

Simon looked at her. 'You know, it's not going to be easy looking after four kittens.'

'Why does everyone keep telling me that?' Mandy exclaimed. 'I don't *care* how hard it is as long as Delilah's kittens are all right!'

The next morning Mandy summoned all her

determination. They would get the kittens to drink the milk. She wondered how the Wards had got on with the feeding since she and James had left the evening before.

One look at Jane Ward's strained face told her all she needed to know. 'They just don't seem to want to drink,' Jane said as she let them in the following morning. 'We've only managed to get a tiny bit down them and they just keep crying all the time. I tried putting a hot water bottle in with them but it made no difference.' She sighed.

Just then Bill came back from taking Tara for a walk. 'Maybe we'll have more luck with all four of us,' he suggested as Tara enthusiastically said hello to Mandy and James.

They managed to get the kittens to take a little bit of the milk but it was hard work. 'Will you be all right tomorrow morning on your own?' Jane asked.

Mandy saw the worry in her eyes and smiled confidently. 'I'm sure we'll be fine,' she said.

When they arrived the next morning they could hear the kittens mewing inside the house. 'Let's hope they're hungry this morning,' James said.

Bill had taken Tara on his rounds to keep her out of Mandy and James's way. 'If you get one of the kittens I'll get the stuff out,' Mandy said, opening the cupboard in the kitchen.

'Which one shall we start with?' James asked.

Mandy considered. 'Daisy,' she decided. 'At least she likes being picked up.'

James went through to the sitting-room while Mandy got the bottles ready. She carefully scooped the formula milk powder out of the bag. It was important to get the measurements just right. She was concentrating hard when she heard James shouting her name. He sounded very agitated.

Mandy looked up in surprise as James came running back into the kitchen. 'Mandy!' he gasped in alarm. 'One of the kittens has gone!'

Mandy stared at him and then ran into the sitting-room. Three little white faces looked up at her. By checking the colour of the nail varnish on the remaining kittens' claws they worked out that Dylan was missing.

'He must have climbed out of the box,' said James.

'But where he's gone?' said Mandy, looking round the room.

James started to look under chairs and behind the settee. 'He's got to be here somewhere,' he said. 'Help me look!'

Together they moved every piece of furniture in the room but there was no sign of Dylan. They looked in the kitchen. They looked in the hall. They turned the sitting-room upside-down.

Mandy's heart was beating fast. 'Where is he?'

'Could he have got outside?' asked James.

Mandy shook her head. 'He's much too small to push the cat flap open.'

James frowned. 'Well, then, he's *got* to be in here somewhere. Kittens don't just disappear.' He went through to the kitchen and looked round to see where a kitten might hide. He looked under the table and round the back of the cooker. Mandy opened all the cupboards and even the fridge but there was no sign of Dylan.

'We've got to think logically,' said James. 'Where would a kitten hide?'

Just then, Blossom appeared through the cat flap and started weaving round Mandy's legs. 'I'd better feed her,' Mandy said, looking down.

'I'll keep looking for Dylan,' said James. 'I'm going to check upstairs. Maybe one of the Wards left the sitting-room door open for a while.'

Mandy mashed Blossom's meat up in her food bowl and poured out some goats' milk from the fridge. *Where was Dylan?* James had said they had to be logical but they'd already covered all the obvious options.

Blossom miaowed.

'Back in a minute,' Mandy called to James. She hurried out of the door but Blossom seemed strangely reluctant to follow her. 'It's your breakfast, come on,' said Mandy. The little cat followed Mandy out but kept looking back towards the house.

'Here we are,' said Mandy, pushing open the door of the shed and putting the bowls down. Blossom settled down to eat. Mandy glanced quickly into the tub. The kittens were lying in a pile, ginger, tabby . . . Mandy frowned. There, in the centre of the pile, was a fluffy white ear and a fluffy white tail. Her eyes widened. It was Dylan!

Blossom hadn't seemed to have noticed the extra kitten in her nest. Mandy quickly scooped Dylan out. The little white kitten nestled warmly in her arms, his blue eyes half-shut, his tail twitching just slightly. Mandy hurried back into the house with the precious bundle in her arms. 'James! I've found him!' she cried as she burst through the back door.

James came running down the stairs. He couldn't believe his eyes. 'Where was he?'

'In the tub with Blossom's kittens.'

'But how did he get there?' asked James, astonished.

Mandy hadn't a clue. 'I'm just glad Blossom didn't notice him in with her kittens,' she said. 'Mother cats can be very protective over their litters.' She kissed Dylan's fluffy white head. 'The most important thing is that he is back now. He must be ready for his breakfast.'

But Dylan was even less co-operative than usual. Mandy held him on her knee while James tried to give him the bottle but Dylan screwed up his face and flatly refused to open his mouth. The milk got into his eyes and ran down on to Mandy's arm. 'We'll have to try later,' said Mandy at last. 'He's just not going to drink at the moment.'

She put Dylan back in the pen. James picked up Desdemona. To their relief, Desdemona and then Daisy and Daniel did drink some of their milk. Dylan, meanwhile, simply curled up in a corner of the pen and went to sleep.

'You don't think he's ill, do you?' James asked when they had finished feeding the other three kittens and had put them down to have a run round the sitting-room.

OFFEE
SUGAR

Mandy picked Dylan up but his breathing and heart rate seemed normal and his gums looked healthy and pink. He didn't seem to be in any distress so Mandy put him back in his corner. 'I think he's OK,' she said cautiously. 'Maybe he'll have some milk later.'

The sun was shining and Mandy and James went outside. They opened the door to Blossom's shed to let in some sunshine Blossom's kittens were playing in the tub, patting at each other's faces and climbing on top of each other.

William put his paws up against the side of the tub and miaowed, his mouth opening to reveal a pink tongue and needle-sharp white teeth. 'He wants to explore,' said Mandy. She looked at James. 'We could take them into the garden. They could play on the grass.'

'But they haven't had any vaccinations yet,' said James.

'They'll be fine in the garden,' said Mandy. 'They just mustn't come into contact with any other cats.' Blossom followed at their feet as they carried the three kittens into the garden. She sniffed each of the kittens when Mandy and James put them on the ground and then lay down a little way off.

The three kittens looked hard at the grass. After staring at it and then sniffing it they took a few cautious steps. Soon Cherry set off to explore a heap of blossom. She rolled over, kicking her tiny legs in the air.

A piece of blossom fluttered towards Peaches. She watched it for a long moment and then clumsily tried to pounce on it. William came to join her and together they patted at it and pounced again, landing in a tangle of legs and tails. Peaches lay down and tried to chew the blossom. Losing interest, William looked round and set off across the grass.

'How far do you think he will go?' James asked.

Mandy wasn't sure. Just as William got about two metres away a car hooted its horn on the road. Terrified, William jumped in the air and scrambled back to the safety of the other kittens. He peered out nervously from behind Cherry, his ears pricked, his eyes wide.

'Poor William,' laughed Mandy. 'I hope that hasn't put him off exploring.' But it obviously hadn't. A few minutes later, William set off again, eager as ever to explore.

Mandy remembered what she had been reading in Simon's book. 'Soon Blossom will start teaching them to hunt,' she said. 'Kittens practise pouncing and stalking and leaping by playing with each other and with their mother. We'll have to bring Delilah's kittens out and bring them up just as Delilah would have done.' The ideas bubbled out of her. 'It will be really good. We can set up hunting games for them and bring all sorts of different foods and make them toys . . .'

'Hang on, Mandy!' James broke in. 'First, we've got to find someone who can feed them when we go back to school next week.'

The wind rushed out of Mandy's sails. She had been so busy thinking about how much fun it would be to bring up the kittens that she had forgotten all about going back to school next week. She had promised the Wards that they would find someone to help.

'They're still going to need feeding every three hours for at least another two weeks,' James pointed out. 'And the Wards have said they can't do it. We've got to think of something, otherwise . . .' His voice trailed off.

'We'll think of something,' said Mandy, her eyes flashing with determination.

Seven

The following morning, Mandy and James unlocked the Wards' back door. Neither of them had thought of anyone who might be able to help with the kittens, although both had been thinking hard. 'There has to be someone,' Mandy said as she pushed the door open. 'If only Gran and Grandad weren't away.'

'If only the kittens were easier to feed,' said James as he followed her into the sitting-room. 'Then it might not be so difficult. But as it is . . .'

'James! 'said Mandy stopping dead. 'Look!'

James's mouth dropped open. There were only two kittens in the run. This time, Mandy didn't need to check the claws to see which kittens were still there. One of the kittens was sitting quietly at the back of the box and the other was standing up against the side asking to be picked up. 'Dylan and Desdemona are missing,' she said in dismay.

'But where have they gone?' James exclaimed.

Mandy looked quickly round. There was no sign of the missing kittens anywhere in the sitting-room.

James hurried to the kitchen and scanned the room. 'They're not here.' He turned to Mandy. 'You don't think they're going to be in Blossom's shed again, do you?'

Mandy stared at him. 'There's only one way to find out!'

They hurried down the path to the shed and looked into the tub. There were five kittens inside.

'Quickly, James!' said Mandy in alarm. 'We've got to get Dylan and Desdemona out before Blossom sees.'

They scooped the two Persian kittens out of the tub just as Blossom trotted in through the shed door.

Dylan and Daisy started to mew. 'Shush, shush,' Mandy said. Blossom stopped dead and looked up at the two white bundles in Mandy and James's arms. Standing up on her hind legs she balanced against Mandy's leg. 'It's all right, Blossom,' Mandy said hastily. 'Don't worry. We're taking them away.'

Blossom trotted after them as they carried the kittens back into the house. She hovered outside the back door.

'That was close,' said James. He frowned as he put Dylan back in the box. 'I just don't understand *how* they are getting out.' He examined the box. 'The sides are just too high.'

Mandy imagined what might have happened if Blossom had found the two white kittens in her nest. 'We can't have them escaping like this. Anything could happen.'

'We've got to find out how they're getting out then,' said James, 'and stop them.' He pushed his glasses up his nose. 'Let's hide and see what they do.'

They went outside and peered in through the sitting-room window. Delilah's kittens mewed loudly but nothing else happened. The minutes ticked by.

'It's a bit cold out here,' said Mandy, shivering and rubbing her arms. Suddenly Blossom entered the sitting-room. 'We'd better stop her,' said Mandy, alarmed. 'We don't want her to go near Delilah's kittens.'

With one quick spring Blossom leaped into the box.

'James! Quick!' gasped Mandy. 'She'll hurt them!'

Mandy and James dashed round to the sitting-room just as Blossom was leaping out of the pen with a kitten hanging in her mouth.

'What's she doing?' James gasped. He was about to grab Blossom when Mandy suddenly stopped him.

'Wait! It's all right!' she said. 'She's just carrying it. Watch!'

They stood like statues as Blossom walked past them with little Dylan swinging from her mouth. She padded across the carpet, into the kitchen and out of the open door. They followed at a safe distance and saw her enter the shed. They opened the door a crack and watched as she gently put Dylan into the tub.

'So *that's* how they've got there,' Mandy said softly. Blossom looked at her and James with an unblinking green stare.

'But why?' said James.

Mandy didn't have an answer. 'Let's see what she does next,' she whispered.

TEA
COFFEE
SUGAR

They moved back into the garden and from the safe distance of the cherry blossom tree watched as Blossom returned into the house and reappeared with Daisy in her mouth and took her to the shed too. Back she went and when she came out she was carrying Desdemona. But this time when she went into the shed, she did not come out again.

'She's left Daniel in the house,' said Mandy, astonished.

Mandy and James crept up to the door and eased it open. Blossom was lying on her side feeding Delilah's three kittens along with her own.

'She's looking after them as if she were their mother,' said James.

'But what about Daniel?' said Mandy.

They went back into the house. Little Daniel was standing all by himself in the run. He was mewing loudly. Mandy scooped him up. 'I don't know what's going on.' she said, mystified. 'I'm going to ring Dad.'

Jean answered the phone and put Mandy on to her father. 'I'll come round,' he said. 'I've got an appointment over near Walton in half an hour. I can call in on the way.'

Ten minutes later, he arrived. Mandy and James took him to the shed where Blossom was feeding the kittens. All six were drinking hungrily. Mr Hope smiled. 'Well, well, well,' he said. 'It looks as though Blossom has decided to foster them. Has she been showing much interest in them?'

'Yes, lots,' said Mandy, rather shamefaced. 'I thought she might be trying to harm them and kept her away.'

'You were right to be cautious,' Mr Hope reassured her. 'But it sounds like she was just worried about them. It's excellent news for the Wards.'

Mandy looked at him. 'So she'll be their foster mother for good? I mean not just today but until Delilah comes back?'

Mr Hope nodded. 'The most important step is over. She's accepted them, even welcomed them, I'd say. Now, she'll bring them up as her own.'

Mandy thought about the one little kitten who was still in the box. 'But what about Daniel?'

Mr Hope rubbed his beard. 'I think Blossom is trying to increase her feeding load little by little, taking one kitten then two and now three. Hopefully, she will take him on as well.' He smiled. 'With all these kittens to feed she's going to need extra food herself. Keep up with the goats' milk too. It's excellent for mothers who are feeding and kittens as well when they get a bit older.'

'We've almost run out,' James said, looking at Mandy. 'We'd better go and get some more.'

'But what about Daniel?' asked Mandy. She couldn't bear to leave the tiny kitten crying by himself in the empty box.

'I'll go,' said James. 'You stay here.'

Mandy waved goodbye to her dad and James and then returned to the sitting-room. Daniel was mewing piteously. Mandy picked him up and, taking him through to the kitchen, made up some formula milk. He was obviously hungry. He accepted quite a bit of the milk before starting to shake his head and struggle. Mandy put down the bottle. He cuddled into the crook of her arm. Looking down at the tiny, vulnerable creature she felt her heart twist. It was so sad seeing him all on his own.

The sound of the cat flap made her look up. Blossom came into the kitchen and headed for the sitting-room. 'Blossom!' Mandy called.

Blossom stopped and looked round. She saw the kitten on Mandy's knee and trotted over. Hardly daring to breathe, Mandy gently placed Daniel on the floor.

Blossom stared up at Mandy. 'Please take him,' Mandy whispered, looking into Blossom's wide green eyes. The cat looked down at the kitten and then, picking him up by the scruff of his neck, turned and trotted towards the door. Mandy's heart leaped. She hurried to the door, watching in delight as Blossom carried Daniel down the path to the shed.

This, Mandy thought, *really is the perfect way to spend a Saturday afternoon.* She and James sat on the grass in the Wards' front garden, watching the kittens play in the sunshine. Bill Ward was standing by the cherry tree. 'I still can't believe she took them all on,' he said, looking at Blossom. The little tabby cat was standing on all fours on Mandy's lap, rubbing her head affectionately against Mandy's shoulder.

Mandy tickled her under the chin. 'You're a very special cat, aren't you, Blossom?' she said She ran a hand down the cat's shiny coat, pleased to find that her fingers no longer bumped painfully over every rib. The kittens were now four weeks old and getting livelier by the day.

'Dylan!' said James as the kitten bounced

sideways up to Desdemona and knocked her over. Peaches hurried over and tried to pounce on their waving tails. She was always trying to catch things. Mandy was sure that she was going to be the first to learn to stalk and pounce properly.

There was a sudden crash from inside the shed. 'What's that?' said Jane Ward in alarm.

Mandy did a quick kitten count. 'Oh no, William's missing!' She jumped to her feet and hurried to the shed. A large box lay upturned on the floor inside. Packets of seeds and gardening gloves were scattered everywhere.

Mandy lifted the box up. 'William!' she exclaimed. The little ginger kitten looked up in surprise and then started to investigate the seeds on the floor.

'He must have pulled it off,' said James, pointing to a strip of fabric that hung from the box. 'I bet he tried to claw at that.'

'Don't let him get to those seeds,' said Bill Ward suddenly. 'They'll be poisonous if he eats one.'

Mandy whisked the kitten off the floor. 'What are we going to do with you?' she scolded him.

Bill scratched his head. 'I should really get this shed cleared up,' he said. 'There's all sorts of things in here that aren't safe, and soon the kittens are going to be able to get out of that tub by themselves.'

'We'll help,' offered Mandy.

It took most of the afternoon to sort out the shed. By the end of it, the Wards' spare bedroom was covered with plastic sheeting and filled with garden equipment. Forks and spades leant against the wardrobe. The dressing-table was covered with cardboard boxes containing packets of seeds, weedkillers and plant food. Pots littered the floor. 'It'll never be the same again!' Jane said, but then she laughed. 'At least the kittens will be safe.'

Back in the shed, Bill leaned a plank against the tub so the kittens could get in and out easily. 'They can explore in here as much as they like now,' he said. 'We can shut the door if we want to keep them in or open it to let them into the garden.'

Mandy changed the newspaper in the tub. 'Perfect!' she said.

Jane picked up little Daisy who was trying to climb up her leg. 'It's going to be so hard when it comes to letting them all go.'

'Have you got homes for them?' Mandy asked.

'We've had lots of inquiries,' Jane told her. 'We're going to keep one ourselves. In another two weeks or so we'll let people come to see them.'

'Which one are you going to keep?' James asked.

Jane Ward looked round at Delilah's kittens and shook her head. 'I don't know. It's impossible to decide.' She looked at the little kitten in her arms. 'Maybe Daisy.'

As Mandy and James started off for home there was a question in Mandy's mind. 'Mrs Ward's got people who want Delilah's kittens,' she said. 'But what are we going to do about Blossom's?'

'I guess we'd better start looking for homes for them,' said James.

'It won't be easy,' said Mandy with a frown, remembering other times when they had tried to find homes for litters of kittens.

'It's going to be even harder to find a home for Blossom,' James pointed out. 'We haven't heard anything from the notices we put up. It really does look as if she was abandoned.'

Mandy's heart sank. James was right. If it was difficult enough finding homes for cute kittens, it was bound to be twice as difficult finding a home for an adult cat.

* * *

Her mind was still on the problem when she sat down for supper that night. Mr Hope had cooked a huge dish of macaroni cheese. He brought it out of the oven, placed it in the centre of the table and picked up an enormous serving spoon.

'I'll serve,' said Mrs Hope quickly.

'It smells delicious, Dad,' said Mandy.

'I suppose I can always have seconds,' said Mr Hope, looking ruefully at the small portion Mrs Hope had put on his plate.

Mandy grinned. 'Not if you want to be able to fit into those jeans for much longer!'

She picked up her fork and started to tell them about looking for homes for Blossom's kittens.

'You could try advertising,' suggested Mr Hope. 'Put up a notice at school maybe? And one in the surgery?'

'There's already so many kittens advertised,' said Mandy, thinking of the surgery notice-board. It had two kitten adverts up already.

'Well, I'll keep my ears open,' promised Mr Hope. 'I suppose a more difficult task is going to be finding a home for Blossom.'

Mandy nodded and then looked hopefully at her parents. 'Mum . . .'

'No,' said Emily Hope, recognising the look. 'Don't even think about asking. You know the rule, Mandy. We can't keep unwanted animals. We'd be overrun.'

Mandy sighed. It was the one rule that her parents were both very strict about. 'Maybe the Wards will keep her,' she said. 'I'll ask.'

Mrs Hope frowned. 'I thought they were planning to keep one of Delilah's kittens?'

Mandy nodded.

'Then I'm sure they won't want another cat. Ask them if you want but don't be too disappointed if the answer's no.' Just then the phone rang. 'I'll get it,' Mrs Hope said, jumping up. She was on call that night.

'Animal Ark. Emily Hope speaking.'

Mandy and her father listened. Was it a work call? Another lambing?

'Right . . . OK . . . I see . . . How much? . . . OK, don't worry, I'll be round as soon as I can.' Mrs Hope put down the phone and hurried back to the table. She was already tying back her long hair. 'That was Lydia Fawcett,' she said, picking up her jumper from the chair. 'One of her goats is ill.'

'Which one? What's the matter?' asked Mandy anxiously.

'Henry, one of her youngsters. He's eaten some rat poison.'

'Oh no!' gasped Mandy.

'I said I'd go up there straight away.'

'Can I come?' asked Mandy, jumping up.

Mrs Hope nodded.

'Good luck,' called Mr Hope as they hurried out of the door.

Eight

It was getting dark by the time Mandy and Mrs Hope reached High Cross Farm. A light shone from the barn. 'Quickly, Mandy!' said Mrs Hope, setting off across the cobbles. Mandy ran after her, her heart thumping. When they opened the barn door they found Lydia sitting in Henry's pen. The little goat's head was hanging down near the straw, his sides heaved in and out, his eyes were half-closed.

'He's been like this for the last half-hour,' Lydia looking up at them with worried eyes.

'Right, I need to see the carton the poison came in,' said Mrs Hope, taking charge. 'Have you got it, Lydia?'

'It's in the kitchen.' Lydia hurried to fetch it while Mrs Hope checked Henry's heart rate and breathing.

Mandy crouched down beside the goat's head. She rubbed his ears but his eyes hardly even flickered in her direction. He bleated unhappily. 'Will he be all right, Mum?'

'It depends on what poison it was that Lydia used,' said Mrs Hope. 'Ah, here she is.'

Lydia reappeared with a large plastic tub. She handed it to Mrs Hope. 'I've never bought rat poison before,' she said and Mandy could see from her eyes how upset she was. 'I bought it this morning and put it down in the feed-room.' She ran a hand through her hair making it stand up at all angles. 'Henry let himself out. I found him in there and it was nearly all gone. That and about half a sack of barley.'

Mrs Hope was inspecting the back of the tub. 'It's OK,' she said quickly. 'It's a warfarin-based poison. Warfarin stops the blood from clotting. It's fatal for rats and mice but doesn't affect goats in nearly the same way. Their digestive system is far stronger. What we need to do is to give him an injection of vitamin K.' She took a syringe out of her bag and started to fill it with a clear liquid.

'So he'll get better?' said Mandy.

Mrs Hope nodded as she injected the vitamin into Henry's neck and patted him. 'I would say he'll be right as rain in twenty-four hours.'

'But he looks so miserable,' said Mandy, looking at the sad little goat with his lowered head and half-shut eyes. As if to prove her right Henry bleated sorrowfully again.

Mrs Hope smiled. 'I think we'll find that that's just a rather nasty tummy-ache from having eaten so much barley. I'll give him something to help that as well but I don't think a tummy-ache is going to threaten his life.'

Lydia looked rather embarrassed. 'Well,' she said, coughing. 'I'm sorry I called you out, Mrs Hope. But I did think it was serious. I won't take up any more of your time.'

'Don't worry,' said Mrs Hope. 'He needed the vitamin K injection anyway.' She smiled at Lydia. 'The most important thing is that he is going to be all right. Now, how about a cup of tea?'

'My pleasure,' said Lydia.

Mandy and her mother followed Lydia down to the farmhouse and into the old-fashioned kitchen. Great, dark, oak beams supported the ceiling. Books littered every surface. Mandy had to move some off a chair to be able to sit down.

Lydia filled a whistling kettle at the shallow sink by the window and put it on the old range to boil.

'So what happened?' Mrs Hope asked curiously. 'How *did* Henry get to the poison?'

Lydia brought over three chipped cups and saucers and sat down. 'It was my fault really. He was in his pen with the safety bolt on,' she sighed. 'I went to catch Houdini and didn't bolt the barn door. By the time I got back with Houdini the barn door was open, the feed-room door was open and Henry had eaten most of the bait on the feed-room floor as well as the sack of barley next to it.'

'But how did he get out of his pen if you had left the safety bolt on?' asked Mandy.

'He must have worked out how to open it with his teeth,' said Lydia. 'I've always known he was a clever one. I'm just going to have to fix a bottom bolt on to his pen door. That should keep him in.'

'So what are you going to do about the rats and mice?' Mrs Hope asked as Lydia poured out the tea.

'Not put rat bait down, that's for sure. It's far too risky with goats like Henry and Houdini around.' Lydia shrugged. 'I just don't know.'

Mrs Hope glanced quickly at Mandy. 'You'll

just have to get a cat, Lydia.'

Mandy stared. She remembered how adamant Lydia had been when she had made the same suggestion a few weeks ago. But perhaps now, after all that had just happened she might change her mind. 'You should, Lydia,' she urged. 'You could have one of Blossom's.' She thought of the large farm and her eyes shone. 'In fact, you could have all three of them!'

Lydia looked rather taken aback. 'Well, you know how I feel about cats, Mandy. I just don't like them.'

'But it's the perfect solution!' Mandy said, the words tumbling eagerly out of her mouth as she tried to convince her old friend. 'How else are you going to keep the rats and mice away? You said they ignored the traps and you can't put poison down again.'

'Well, maybe,' Lydia said doubtfully.

'And Blossom's kittens are not at all cold and unfriendly,' Mandy said, remembering what Lydia had said about cats. 'They're cuddly and adorable and love people.'

'Why don't you go and have a look at the kittens and see what you think?' suggested Mrs Hope.

'Then they could all have a home together!' said Mandy.

Lydia quickly shook her head. 'I certainly wouldn't want more than two.'

Mandy's face fell but then she brightened. At least two of the kittens would have a good home and it might not be so bad finding a home for just one little kitten. 'Come and see them,' she pleaded. 'You'll love them.'

By the time Mandy and her mother left, Lydia had agreed to come and see the kittens the following weekend. 'They'll be five weeks old by then,' said Mandy.

'And when would they be ready to go to their new homes?' Lydia asked cautiously. 'Not that I'm promising anything, you realise.'

'From about eight weeks old,' said Mrs Hope.

Lydia nodded rather half-heartedly. 'Well, I'll come and see but, as I said, I'm absolutely not promising.'

The following Saturday, James and Mandy arrived early at the Wards' house. They were determined to make the kittens look as beautiful as possible before Lydia came.

'Surely when she sees them she won't be able to choose two and leave just one without a home,' said Mandy.

They put Delilah's kittens out in the garden

and then checked William, Peaches and Cherry over carefully. All three kittens had soft, shiny coats and bright eyes. Blossom watched as Mandy and James inspected for fleas.

'Not a thing,' said James. He put down Cherry and she trotted off to play with William. Peaches joined them and together they chased the blossom blowing across the grass beneath the tree. Mandy noticed that they had stopped falling over as much when they pounced. Sometimes Peaches could even manage a running jump and a spring.

'Look at William!' said Mandy. William had discovered a snail and was licking it. Whenever any of the kittens encountered something new at the moment they tried to taste it. Mandy was very relieved that they had cleared out the shed so thoroughly. It would be awful if the kittens tried to lick anything that was poisonous.

Blossom walked over to James and rubbed her head affectionately against his leg; then, sitting up on her back legs, she begged for attention. 'I still can't believe she's a stray,' said Mandy, bending down to stroke her. 'She's so friendly now.'

William and Desdemona came trotting over. They tried to pounce on Blossom's tail. She shook them off and stalked away.

'She's just starting to get fed up with them,' said Mandy. 'She'll stop letting them suckle in a week or two.'

James watched as the two kittens charged after Blossom and jumped on her tail again, clawing at it and chewing it with their needle-sharp teeth. 'I can see why!'

Blossom took refuge up the cherry blossom tree. The garden gate creaked open. It was Lydia. Mandy and James jumped to their feet. 'Hi,' said Mandy running over.

'So, where are these kittens then?' Lydia said, looking around rather dubiously.

'Over here,' said Mandy, taking Lydia over to the tree. She held her breath as Lydia looked down at the bundles of white, ginger and tabby fluff. 'The white ones are Delilah's, they've all got homes.'

Peaches came stalking over and pounced on Lydia's foot with her claws out. Lydia laughed and picked her up. Peaches miaowed loudly.

'Well?' said Mandy.

There was a long pause. Lydia looked down at the little kitten in her arms. Peaches blinked up at her, her head on one side. Closing her eyes she rubbed her face against Lydia's chest.

Lydia looked at Mandy and James and her face broke into a smile. 'Maybe I do need a cat,' she said.

Mandy threw her arms round her, being careful not to crush Peaches at the same time. 'Oh, Lydia! That's brilliant!'

'Which one?' James said eagerly.

Lydia looked down at Peaches in her arms. 'Do you think this one could catch a few mice?'

'Definitely!' Mandy enthused. 'She's brilliant at pouncing. I think she'll be great at hunting when she gets older.'

'Then I'll have her.' Lydia looked over the other kittens. 'He looks like a character,' she said, pointing to William who was halfway down the garden, lying on his back and wrestling with a daffodil.

James grinned. 'He certainly is.'

'Then I'll have him too,' decided Lydia. 'They can keep each other company.'

James scooped up little Cherry. 'That only leaves Cherry,' he said. 'She'll be all by herself.'

But Lydia wasn't to be swayed. She shook her head firmly. 'Two's enough for me.'

Mandy sighed. Her plan of having all three of them in one home didn't look like it was going to work out. Still, at least Peaches and

William would be together and she would be able to see them whenever she went up to High Cross Farm. That was something. She picked William up and brought him over. 'He's quite bossy,' she said. 'He likes having his own way.'

Lydia laughed. 'Just like the goats.' She took William off Mandy. 'I can see you and I will get on just fine,' she said to the little ginger kitten. She looked down at the two kittens in her arms. 'Cats,' she said in surprise. 'I'm going to have two cats!'

When Mandy got back to Animal Ark that afternoon she went into the residential unit. Delilah was the only patient in and she looked very bored. Mandy opened the cage and took her out. 'You'll be going home soon,' she said, cuddling the white cat. She knew it was hard for any animal to have to stay in a cage and rest, but cats in particular really hated being confined. She decided to groom her and, finding a brush, sat down on the floor.

Mrs Hope looked round the door. 'I thought I heard you come in,' she said. She looked at the cat. 'How's Delilah today?'

'Bored,' said Mandy.

Mrs Hope came over and tickled Delilah's

ears. 'Bill and Jane are coming to visit her tomorrow so hopefully that will cheer her up. Anyway, how did it go with Lydia today? Has she decided to have one of the kittens?'

'She's taking two,' grinned Mandy. 'She loved them. She chose Peaches and William. So it's just Cherry and Blossom who need homes now.'

Mrs Hope frowned. 'Maybe you should ring up Betty Hilder at the Animal Sanctuary. Warn her that you may be bringing them in. It will give her a chance to start looking for homes for them.'

'But the Wards don't mind having them in their shed,' said Mandy quickly. 'If Blossom and Cherry go up to the Sanctuary they will have to go into a cage.'

'The cages at the sanctuary are quite roomy. It will be easier for Betty to find a home for Cherry while she's still a little kitten.'

'It won't be easy to find a home for Blossom,' Mandy argued. 'No one wants adult cats. Blossom may be in there for ages. She'll hate it!'

Mrs Hope sighed. 'It is more difficult to find homes for adult cats,' she admitted. 'Still, you can't expect the Wards to let Blossom stay in their shed forever. The sooner Betty knows, the better.'

'But, Mum . . .'

'No buts, Mandy.' Mrs Hope's eyes were firm. 'Give Betty a ring tomorrow. It's the only sensible thing to do.'

Nine

Mandy sat at the kitchen table at Animal Ark and tried to make a list of all the people who might give Blossom a home. It wasn't going very well – in fact, it didn't have any names on it at all. She sighed and chewed the end of her pen. There had to be *someone* she knew who wanted a cat.

Blossom deserved a loving home. She had so many endearing habits – the way she would roll in the blossom, the way she would sit up on her back legs and beg for food and attention, the way she would rub her head against your hand, purring loudly. It was hard to imagine that anyone could have abandoned her.

Mrs Hope came into the kitchen. She was carrying Delilah. 'Jane and Bill are coming round,' she said. 'I thought I'd bring Delilah into the sitting-room. It will be more comfy for them in there. Dad's been called out to a calving.' She put Delilah down. 'Have you rung Betty yet?'

Mandy shook her head.

'Mandy . . .'

'I will, Mum!'

Just then the phone rang. 'I'll get it,' Mandy exclaimed, seizing the chance to escape. 'Hello,' she said quickly. 'Welford 703267.'

'Good morning, this is Lydia Fawcett speaking.' Lydia had only recently had a telephone connected to High Cross Farm and always sounded rather formal on the phone.

Mandy smiled. 'Hi, Lydia. Do you want to speak to Mum?'

'Actually, no. I was ringing about the two kittens.' Lydia cleared her throat. 'I happened to be in town yesterday and while I was there I bought two baskets, some toys and two bowls. I was wondering if there is any other equipment you would suggest I purchase?'

'I don't think so,' said Mandy, rather taken aback. 'You sound like you've got everything.'

'If I take on a responsibility to an animal I like to see it through,' said Lydia stiffly. 'All the animals at High Cross Farm are looked after to the best of my capabilities.'

Mandy smiled. She knew Lydia well enough to realise that underneath the stiff and formal exterior Lydia was secretly rather excited at the prospect of having the two kittens coming to live at High Cross Farm. William and Peaches really couldn't be going to a better home. 'I'm so glad you're having the kittens, Lydia,' she said. 'They'll be so happy with you.'

There was a pause. When Lydia spoke again her tone had softened slightly. 'I am rather looking forward to having them,' she admitted.

As Mandy put down the phone she heard her mother letting the Wards in. Mandy hurried through to the sitting-room to see Delilah's reaction. As always when Delilah saw them, her bored expression vanished. She rubbed against their legs, purring non-stop. 'Oh, Delilah,' said Jane Ward, kneeling on the floor beside her. 'You are glad to see us, aren't you?'

Bill rubbed her ears. 'There's a good lass. We've been missing you.' Delilah's purrs got even louder as she rubbed her head against his face.

'She's getting much better,' Mrs Hope said. 'We're very pleased with her. If it wasn't for the kittens I would let her come home with you now. However, it is better to be safe than sorry. Her bones are still at a delicate stage in the healing process. Even though it means her being bored here, I think she should stay until the kittens have gone to their new homes.'

'We've decided we're going to keep Daisy,' said Jane. 'Will Delilah be all right, when she does come back, if Daisy wants to play?'

'I'll want you to keep a careful eye on the pair of them at first,' said Mrs Hope. 'But it should be fine.'

Jane frowned. 'Actually I've been meaning to ask you a question about Daisy. We've heard you can have cats microchipped so they can be traced if they are lost or stolen. What do you think about it?'

'Good idea,' agreed Mrs Hope. 'Have you had Delilah done?' Mrs Ward shook her head. 'Well, then I'd recommend that they were both done.'

'How dangerous is it?' asked Bill cautiously.

'Not at all,' said Mrs Hope. 'All it involves is inserting a tiny microchip in the back of the cat's neck and it means that if they ever get lost and are picked up by a big animal shelter or taken into a police station then you can be contacted. The microchip is tiny, only about the size of a grain of rice, and yet when it is scanned into a computer it reveals the owner's details. I think all pets should be done. It would prevent an awful lot of heartache.'

Mandy stared at her mother as a sudden thought struck her. 'Mum! What about Blossom? We've never checked to see if she has a microchip.'

Mrs Hope frowned. 'No, we haven't.' She shrugged. 'I guess it might be worth a try.'

'Can we go and get her now and see?' asked Mandy. If Blossom did have a microchip then her owner could be traced and the little cat wouldn't have to be rehomed.

Mrs Hope looked at the Wards. 'Don't worry about us,' said Bill cheerfully. 'We'll wait here and spend some time with Delilah, if that's all right with you?'

Mrs Hope nodded. 'Of course. We won't be long.'

Mandy picked up a plastic cat carrier from the office and jumped into the car. 'Now don't build your hopes up,' Mrs Hope warned. 'Not that many cat owners have their cats microchipped.' But Mandy didn't want to listen to her mother's practical warning. 'Can I ring up James on the mobile?' she asked. She knew James would be as excited as she was.

Mrs Hope smiled and nodded. James arranged to meet them at Animal Ark so that he could be there when Mrs Hope tested for the microchip. They collected Blossom with no trouble at all, shutting the kittens in the shed so they would be safe until Blossom was returned.

James was waiting at the bottom of the Animal Ark driveway. He cycled up after them. 'You really think she might have a microchip?' he asked Mandy as she jumped out of the car.

Mandy nodded. 'Fingers crossed!'

The Wards joined them in the consulting room to see if Blossom had had a microchip implanted. They stood to one side with James while Mandy held Blossom firmly on the table. Mrs Hope took a piece of equipment out of a drawer. It looked just like a bar-code scanner at a supermarket checkout. Mrs Hope ran it over Blossom's back and neck. 'If she has a microchip then we will hear a bleep,' she explained.

There was no sound. 'Try again,' urged Mandy. She knew that sometimes the chip could move slightly. She crossed her fingers tightly. For one awful moment she thought her hopes were going to have been in vain and then, *bleep*!

Mandy jumped in the air with excitement. 'She's got one!' she cried, grabbing James and hugging him. 'There it is!' James went rather red and she hastily let go of him. 'Mum! We can find Blossom's owners!' she cried

Mrs Hope kissed her. 'You were right, love. Well done.' She noted down the microchip number the scanner had picked up. 'Each microchip has a different number,' she said, turning to the Wards. 'Now all we need to do is ring up the database holders with this number

and they should be able to find out Blossom's owner's contact details.'

Mandy hugged Blossom impatiently as her mother telephoned the helpline. Mrs Hope reported Animal Ark's authorisation code and then the number on Blossom's chip.

'What happens now?' Mandy asked as her mother put down the phone.

'Now they contact the owner,' said Mrs Hope.

'And then the owner will contact Animal Ark?' asked James.

Mrs Hope nodded. 'But only if the details on the database are still correct – sometimes people forget to update them if they move house or if circumstances change.' She looked carefully at Mandy and James. 'Now I don't want you getting your hopes up. Even if the details are correct and they do reach Blossom's owner then it is just possible that they might not actually want her back.'

Mandy stared. 'What do you mean? Of course they'll want her.'

Mrs Hope shook her head. 'We don't know that for sure. They might have abandoned her on purpose.'

Mandy looked down at the little tabby cat in her arms. It was hard to believe that anyone would do such a thing, but then she knew that not everyone felt the way she did about animals. She kissed Blossom's head and then met James's gaze. There was nothing they could do now but wait.

Monday and Tuesday passed slowly. There was no word from Blossom's owners. By Tuesday evening a seed of doubt started to grow in Mandy's mind. Maybe her mum was right. Maybe Blossom's owners didn't want her any more. The wonderful hopeful feelings began to slowly fizzle away. *It's beginning to look as if we're going to have to find a home for Blossom after all,* she thought, getting out her bike on Wednesday morning.

She called goodbye to her dad who was just going into the surgery, adjusted her rucksack on her back and set off down the drive.

'Mandy!' She braked and turned. Mr Hope was waving from the surgery door.

'What?' she called.

'There's a message on the answerphone I think you might want to hear. It's from Blossom's owner!'

Dropping her bike on the gravel, Mandy raced up the drive and into the surgery. She pressed the answerphone's play button eagerly. 'One message. Wednesday, seven fifty-seven a.m.,' said the computerised voice. Mr Hope came up behind her. Mandy glanced at him with excited eyes.

'Umm, hello,' came a female voice. 'My name is Mrs Stanley. I've just had a message that you have found my cat. I can come round and collect her today about five o'clock. I hope that's OK.' There was a pause. 'I'd almost given up hope,' the voice continued. Mandy had the impression that the woman leaving the message was suddenly fighting back tears. 'I've been looking for her for four months, you see. We moved house and . . . well, I can tell you when I see you. Bye.'

Mandy stared at the answerphone, caught between elation and dismay. Mrs Stanley sounded like she loved Blossom very much but now she wanted to come and take her away that day! 'What about the kittens!' Mandy exclaimed, turning to her father. 'Delilah's kittens are too young to manage without Blossom. They're not weaned yet. She can't take Blossom away tonight!'

'I'm afraid she can, Mandy,' Mr Hope said. 'She is Blossom's owner, after all.'

Mandy started to shake her head. 'No!'

Mr Hope squeezed her arm. 'Come on. Mrs Stanley may be perfectly reasonable about it and agree to let Blossom stay for a bit longer.'

'She should have left a number!' said Mandy. 'She's going to arrive and not know about Blossom's kittens. She might not want them.' Her eyes widened as an even worse thought crossed her mind. 'Or she might want to keep them *all* and then what will Lydia do?' She stared at her father in dismay.

'It's not going to do any good worrying about it,' Mr Hope said reasonably. 'Go on, off to school. Everything will work out, you'll see.'

But what if it doesn't? thought Mandy as she got back on to her bike. *What if Mrs Stanley insists on taking Blossom, Cherry, Peaches and William away?* A lump formed in her throat.

'Hi!' called James as she cycled up. As soon as he saw her face he frowned. 'What's up?'

Mandy had to fight back the tears as she explained, James stared at her in horror. 'She can't take away Blossom. Whatever would the Wards do?'

'Someone would have to look after the kittens,' Mandy said. 'But you know how difficult it is and, anyway, they're at such an important stage in their development. They need a mother.' She looked at him desperately. 'James, we can't let this happen.'

'But what can we do?'

Mandy shook her head. She was thrilled that Blossom wouldn't have to go to the Animal Sanctuary, but she couldn't shake off a feeling of impending doom. 'We'll think of something,' she said, determinedly.

But, for once, Mandy was at a complete loss for ideas. Her dad was right. Mrs Stanley had every right to take Blossom and her kittens away if she wanted to. As five o'clock drew near, Mandy and James waited uneasily in the reception of Animal Ark. Jean tapped at the computer, smiling at them whenever she looked up.

Mandy tidied up the leaflets and nervously straightened the pile of magazines. James watched out of the window. Mrs Hope was in the treatment room with a beagle puppy and his owner but she popped her head out. 'Any sign of Mrs Stanley?'

James shook his head. Mandy walked up and down the waiting-room.

'There's a car coming,' James said, a few

minutes later. 'Do you recognise it?' Mandy rushed to the window and shook her head. They watched as the woman got out. She was about Mrs Hope's age and was wearing a long navy dress. James raised his eyebrows. 'What do you reckon, Mandy? She doesn't exactly look like a heartless monster.'

'But what if she is?' Mandy gabbled nervously.

The door opened and the woman came in.

'Umm, hello,' she said, running a hand rather nervously through her short dark hair. She looked from Mandy to James and then at Jean. She was obviously unsure who to talk to. 'I've come for my cat. She's here, I believe. My name's Janice Stanley.'

Mandy took a deep breath and introduced herself. 'My parents are the vets here,' she explained. 'Your cat isn't here, she's staying at a house nearby. James and I have been helping to look after her.'

'But you have got her and she is all right?'

Mandy nodded and saw the relief light up in Mrs Stanley's eyes. 'Actually,' Mandy cast a look in James's direction for moral support, 'she's had kittens.' She watched carefully for Mrs Stanley's reaction.

'Kittens!' she gasped. Mandy and James

nodded. 'Goodness, I don't know what to say.' She rubbed her forehead.

Just then Mrs Hope came out with the beagle and his owner. She realised straight away who Mrs Stanley was and came over and introduced herself.

'I've just been told about the kittens,' Mrs Stanley said, still sounding rather shocked.

'*All* the kittens?' Mrs Hope asked with a look at Mandy. Mandy shook her head. Mrs Stanley looked at them in some alarm.

Mrs Hope hastily explained. 'Your cat's been a foster mother for four Persian kittens as well as her own three kittens, Mrs Stanley. The Persians' mother was in a car accident and is recovering here in our residential unit. Before the accident your cat was living in the owner's garden shed and after the accident she took it upon herself to foster the kittens.'

'Oh,' said Mrs Stanley faintly.

The words burst from Mandy. 'But they're only five weeks old and still really need her. Please don't take her away just yet! Please let her stay another two weeks!'

Mrs Stanley looked as if she didn't know what to say.

Mrs Hope smiled at her. 'I know this must all

come as a bit of a surprise,' she said. 'And I'm sure at the moment you just want to see your cat. Why don't you follow me in your car? It's not far.' Mrs Stanley nodded gratefully.

In the car, James looked at Mandy. 'Well, what do you think?'

'I don't know,' said Mandy with a frown. 'She seemed all right but she didn't say much when I asked her whether Blossom could stay.'

Mrs Hope shook her head as she started the engine. 'You hardly gave the poor woman a chance, Mandy. She was completely taken aback and I hardly blame her. Her cat's been missing for four months, she turns up to collect her only to be told that she's had kittens, she's fostering another litter and that you don't want her to take her away just yet.'

Mandy felt her face go a bit pink. 'I guess so.'

They arrived at the Wards to find Bill and Jane waiting anxiously in the garden. Mrs Hope had phoned them earlier in the day to tell them the news. Mandy and James ran to meet them.

'What's she like?' Mrs Ward asked Mandy. 'Do you think she will let Blossom stay?'

Before Mandy could reply, Mrs Stanley arrived. She came through the gate and crossed the grass eagerly towards them. She suddenly stopped dead. 'Blossom!' she whispered, staring at the tabby cat sitting in a patch of late afternoon sunlight. 'Blossom, is it really you?'

'How did you know that was what we called her?' Mandy asked.

James nudged her to be quiet and nodded towards Blossom. The little cat had stiffened at the sound of her owner's voice. Her tabby ears pricked and the next minute she was bounding over the grass, heading straight as an arrow for Mrs Stanley.

Mrs Stanley bent down and opened her arms. The little cat put her paws up on Mrs Stanley's shoulder and started rubbing her head frantically against her cheek.

'Oh, Blossom!' cried Mrs Stanley. 'I'm so glad to see you.'

As she straightened up, Mandy repeated the question that was burning on her lips. 'But how did you know we called her Blossom?'

'I didn't,' said Mrs Stanley. 'That's her name. You mean, you called her Blossom, too?'

Mandy explained how the name had come about.

'But that's just why I called her Blossom in the first place,' said Mrs Stanley, in astonishment. 'I saw her rolling in the blossom when she was a tiny kitten.'

Mandy grinned. 'No wonder she seemed to learn it so quickly!'

'I think it's time for some human introductions,' said Mrs Hope. She introduced the Wards.

'It's our cat, Delilah, who was in the accident,' Jane explained. 'Blossom's been helping us out by looking after the kittens.'

'Jane and Bill started feeding Blossom when she first came into the garden,' said Mrs Hope.

'Well, we noticed she was a bit thin,' said Bill. 'And expecting kittens too.'

Mandy noticed Mrs Stanley smiling gratefully. 'Mr and Mrs Ward have really been wonderful,' she said. 'They gave Blossom a home and made friends with her and helped when she was ill having her kittens.' She glanced at James and he took the hint.

'They even cleared out all the things from their garden shed and put them into their spare room so that Blossom and the kittens would be quite safe,' he said.

'You've all been so kind,' said Mrs Stanley looking round. 'I really can't thank you enough.'

'The kittens will be completely weaned in

another couple of weeks,' said Mandy, her eyes pleading with Mrs Stanley. 'If Blossom could just stay till then?'

Mrs Stanley's eyes were torn. 'I know they need Blossom, it's just . . .' She looked down at Blossom in her arms. 'I've missed her so much. We were moving house from Walton when she disappeared. I searched everywhere, came back every day but there was no sign of her. I was starting to give up hope when I got the message. I know I should leave her here, I know it's the right thing to do,' her voice choked up a bit, 'but I just don't know if I can bear to do it.'

Mandy glanced anxiously at James. Somehow they had to make Mrs Stanley see how important it was that Blossom stayed.

'Look out! One of the kittens has got a bee!' Mrs Hope exclaimed.

Everyone looked round, alarmed. Over by the tree, a large bumble-bee was crawling slowly across the grass. Daisy was staring at it, fascinated. She patted at it with her paw. The bee buzzed angrily. Daisy put her head on one side. 'She's going to try to eat it!' exclaimed Mandy, recognising the expression on Daisy's face.

'Someone stop her!' gasped Mrs Stanley.

Before anyone could move, Blossom had twisted out of Mrs Stanley's arms, streaked across the grass and reached the little kitten. With one swipe of her paw she knocked Daisy firmly out of harm's way. Daisy rolled over on to her back. The bumble-bee crawled safely away.

Everyone sighed with relief. 'That was lucky,' said Mrs Hope. 'If Daisy had swallowed the bee there's a chance it would have stung her and the swelling might have blocked up her airway.'

Mandy raced over and scooped up Daisy. 'Oh, Daisy, you silly kitten, that was very dangerous,' she said. 'You mustn't play with bees.' She brought her back to where the others were standing.

'The bee must have been waking up after the winter. That's why it was going so slowly,' said Mrs Hope.

'At least Daisy's all right,' said Mandy, cuddling the little kitten.

'Can I hold her?' asked Mrs Stanley rather shyly. Mandy handed Daisy to her. Mrs Stanley looked down at the kitten in her arms. 'I guess I can't take Blossom away, can I?' she said. 'They really do need her.'

Mandy felt her heart leap. 'It's only for

another two weeks, Mrs Stanley.'

'And you can come and visit,' said Jane Ward, her face lighting up with delight. 'Any time you want.'

'It really will make a tremendous difference, Mrs Stanley,' Mrs Hope put in warmly.

Mrs Stanley cheered up. 'At least at the end of it, I'll have Blossom and three kittens to take home. That's certainly something to look forward to.'

'What will you do with the kittens?' asked James. 'Will you keep them all?'

Mandy held her breath and waited for the answer.

'I'd love to but I really haven't the room. I'll keep just one.' Mrs Stanley looked to where little Cherry was rolling in the blossom on the grass. 'And I don't think I'll have to think too hard about which one it will be.'

'Cherry?' said Mandy, following her gaze.

'She looks just like Blossom did at that age.' Mrs Stanley smiled. 'Don't worry though, I'll make sure I find good homes for the other two.'

'But we've already found them a brilliant home!' The words burst out of Mandy. 'A home together on a farm.'

Mrs Stanley looked rather surprised. 'Oh.'

'It was all arranged before Mandy had the idea of looking to see whether Blossom had a microchip,' said Mrs Hope quickly. 'It really would be an excellent home for them, Mrs Stanley, if you don't have any definite plans.'

Mandy waited anxiously. Mrs Stanley smiled. 'Well, in that case, I'm certainly not going to argue. After all, the most important thing is that all the kittens are happy.'

Smiling broadly, Jane invited everyone in for a cup of tea. As the adults set off into the house, James nudged Mandy. 'So, Mrs Stanley's a monster then?' he said slyly.

Mandy grinned and, in reply, picked up a handful of blossom and stuck it down his back.

Mrs Hope drove the four-wheel drive slowly back through the village. 'I can't believe it's worked out so well,' said Mandy contentedly. 'We don't have to say goodbye to Blossom just yet, after all.'

'Delilah's kittens will have her as a mum for a bit longer,' said James.

'Peaches and William are going to go and live at High Cross Farm,' said Mandy.

'And Delilah is well on the way to making a full recovery,' put in Mrs Hope.

Mandy looked happily at James. 'Isn't life great?'

Cats in the Caravan

One

Mandy Hope gazed down at Dylan, the sick puppy who had been brought into Animal Ark the day before. 'You're being such a brave boy,' she said softly, stroking the puppy's head.

The young Bernese Mountain dog, who was recovering from an operation on his spine, looked up at Mandy with soulful brown eyes. He was only four months old and still had his fluffy puppy coat. Mandy smoothed his silky black ears and lightly touched each of his sweet tan eyebrows.

Just then, the door opened. Emily Hope, Mandy's mother, came in. 'How is he?' she asked quietly. Her long red hair was tied back but, as usual, soft strands were escaping round her face.

'He's still not moving,' Mandy replied, her blue eyes full of worry. 'He *is* going to get better, isn't he, Mum?'

Mrs Hope leaned into Dylan's cage and gently examined the row of stitches that ran down the back of the pup's neck. 'I hope so, love. I really do,' she replied. 'But it's going to be a few days before your dad and I know whether the operation has been a success.'

'What would have happened if you hadn't operated?' Mandy asked, looking at the doleful puppy.

'His condition would have deteriorated quickly,' her mum explained. 'He had a cyst – a swelling – growing in his spine. It was stopping his muscles from getting the right messages from his brain. If we hadn't operated, then it would have got bigger, eventually paralysing him.' She stroked the puppy gently as she spoke. 'It was a complicated operation but if we hadn't done it then Dylan would have had to be put down. At least, this way, we've given him a chance.'

Mandy nodded, feeling a little better.

'Let's leave him to rest, love,' Mrs Hope said. 'There's nothing more we can do now.'

Giving Dylan a kiss on his head, Mandy shut the cage door. She followed her mum out of the residential unit where all the Animal Ark patients that were too ill to go home were kept. Animal Ark, an old stone cottage with a modern red-brick extension, was both Mandy's home and her parents' veterinary surgery.

'Now, didn't you say something about visiting Wilfred Bennett and Matty this morning?' Mrs Hope said as they went into the cosy, oak-beamed kitchen.

'Yes,' said Mandy, taking off the white coat she always wore when she was helping with the patients. She cheered up slightly as she thought of her plans for the first day of spring half-term. 'I'm meeting James at the Fox and Goose crossroads at ten o'clock, then we're going on to Wilfred's house.' Wilfred Bennett had once run the local riding-school. A short while ago, his wife, Rose, had died and Wilfred had been forced to sell up. He had sold all of the horses apart from Rose's grey mare, Matty, who was Mandy's favourite.

'Well, give Matty a hug from me,' Mrs Hope said.

'And an apple?' said Mandy, looking hopefully at the large fruitbowl on the kitchen table.

Her mum smiled. 'And an apple,' she said.

'Thanks, Mum,' Mandy said, pulling on a jacket and stuffing the biggest apple into her pocket.

Mrs Hope glanced at her watch. 'Did you just say you were meeting James at ten?'

Mandy nodded.

Mrs Hope raised her eyebrows. 'Well, you'd better get a move on. It's five minutes past already.'

'Oh no!' Mandy gasped. She had been so busy with Dylan that she had completely lost track of time. 'James'll go mad!'

'Bye!' Mrs Hope laughed, as Mandy grabbed her scarf and ran out of the door.

It only took Mandy a few seconds to jump on to her bike. She pedalled furiously, past the wooden sign that said 'Animal Ark Veterinary Surgery' and down the lane that led to the main road. A biting February wind blew Mandy's short, dark blonde hair back from her face, but she was cycling so hard that she hardly felt the cold.

As she got near to the crossroads she saw James Hunter, her best friend, and Blackie, his Labrador, waiting by the signpost. James was standing by his bike, his glasses halfway down his nose as usual.

'What time do you call this?' he said, pretending to be indignant, as Mandy braked beside him.

'Sorry,' she panted, her cheeks flushed from the wind and exercise. She patted Blackie who was leaping round her ecstatically. 'I was with Dylan.'

'Oh, how is he?' James asked quickly. Mandy had rung him up the night before to tell him all about the puppy's operation.

'Still not moving,' Mandy replied. Blackie jumped up at her, almost sending her and her bike flying. 'Blackie!' she said sternly. 'Down!'

Blackie backed off. Mandy quickly stroked him to show that she didn't mean to be cross with him. She had known Blackie ever since he had been a tiny puppy and she adored him. As she scratched his ears, he thumped his tail against the ground. 'He's lively today,' she said to James.

'He hasn't been for a walk yet,' James said. He looked rather sheepish. 'Actually I overslept – I only got here about a minute ago.'

'And you let *me* feel guilty!' Mandy exclaimed, reaching out to punch his arm.

James dodged and grinned. 'I couldn't resist it! Come on, let's go. If we cycle fast it might tire Blackie out.'

They cycled along the hilly road that led out of Welford village with Blackie bounding happily beside them. The tree branches were still bare but along the roadside there were clumps of nodding white snowdrops and the first early daffodils could just be seen pushing their green tips out of the ground.

Wilfred Bennett's small stone cottage stood by the roadside just outside the village. The rolling land behind it that had once been Wilfred's riding-school was now fenced off and a sign by the entrance leading into it read 'Rose of Yorkshire Campsite'.

'I wonder when the campsite will be opening again for the summer,' Mandy said to James as they leaned their bikes against the fence.

'Maybe Wilfred will know,' James said. He called Blackie who was sniffing in some long grass. Blackie trotted over and sat obediently to have his lead clipped on to his collar. 'There, you're not naughty all the time, are you?' James said, glancing at Mandy.

She grinned. 'Just most of it!'

They went to Wilfred's front door and banged the horse-shaped brass knocker. A few moments later, the door opened and Wilfred Bennett's kind old face peered out.

'Hi, Wilfred,' Mandy said. 'We've come to visit.'

Wilfred's weather-beaten cheeks creased even more as he smiled broadly. 'Well, that's what I call a coincidence,' he said in his deep Yorkshire accent. 'I was going to give you two a ring this morning. I've got a bit of a problem and I thought you might be able to help.'

'What is it?' James asked curiously.

But before Wilfred could reply, a thin grey cat came trotting round the corner of the cottage. Mandy looked at it in surprise. Wilfred didn't have a cat.

Suddenly Blackie spotted the cat too. With an excited bark, he lunged forward, almost pulling James off his feet.

The cat froze for half a second and then, like lightning, it streaked across the road and vanished

under the far hedge in a blur of dark grey fur.

'Blackie!' James cried. 'How many times have I told you not to do that?'

Blackie sat down again, looking contrite. But Mandy grinned as she noticed a slight wag in the Labrador's tail. She turned to Wilfred. 'Whose cat is that?' she asked. 'I haven't seen it before.'

'I don't rightly know, lass,' Wilfred replied. 'But it's my guess she was one of Arthur Oldfield's cats.'

'Oh! Poor thing!' Mandy gasped. She had heard her parents talking about Arthur Oldfield a while ago. He had been a bit of a recluse, his only company being the handful of pedigree British Blue cats he had kept. But last summer he had died, and his distraught pets had run off and begun to live wild.

Wilfred nodded gravely. 'I've seen several grey cats like his round here,' he added. 'That one turned up yesterday and made a home in my backyard.' He rubbed his chin. 'I put a bit of food out for her,' he said. 'But the problem is, I'm allergic to cats, so I'd rather she was found another home. That's why I was going to ring you. I thought you might be able to help,' he explained.

'Of course we will,' Mandy said immediately. She and James had often rescued stray animals before – dogs, cats, and all sorts of wildlife. But her parents had a strict rule about taking in stray animals at Animal Ark. 'We have enough animal responsibilities as it is,' her mum always said. However, Mandy was sure that kind-hearted Betty Hilder, who ran the nearby animal sanctuary, would be happy to take the cat.

Already Mandy's mind was whirling, but before she could say anything else, Wilfred spoke again. 'Before you do anything, lass, I think there's something else you should see . . .' he said.

Exchanging surprised glances, Mandy and James followed Wilfred into his backyard. What was he going to show them?

Wilfred's backyard was tiny, little more than a square of concrete containing a dustbin and a coal bunker. He led them across the yard to where a narrow passageway ran between the cottage and the campsite fence. He nodded at the passageway. 'There,' he said.

Mandy stepped forward. The passageway was half covered by the overhanging roof of the cottage and at the far end it was shadowy and dimly lit. She could just make out a pile of old newspapers and there in the newspapers were . . .

'Kittens!' she gasped.

Huddled together in a makeshift newspaper nest were three small kittens. Two were grey-and-white and one was black with a white triangle on his chest. They crouched together, their eyes blinking. From the size of them, Mandy guessed they must be three to four weeks old. She swung round. 'Are they the grey cat's?'

'Aye,' Wilfred said, nodding. 'She brought them here yesterday. It's my guess she was looking for somewhere safe for them but they can't stay here – it's too cold. They need to be inside.'

Blackie pulled on his lead, whining in his eagerness to go and investigate the kittens. They shrank back nervously against the paper, making tiny mewing sounds.

'I'd better keep Blackie away from them,' James said quickly. 'He might scare them.'

Mandy nodded. 'I'll see how friendly they are,' she said. She edged cautiously into the narrow passageway. The kittens drew back a little. Keen not to alarm them, Mandy crouched down and crawled slowly on her knees towards them. The floor was damp but Mandy didn't care. Her eyes were fixed on the three kittens.

As she drew closer she could see their markings more clearly. Both grey-and-white kittens had grey heads and white chests but one was smaller than the other and had a white smudge on its muzzle and white front legs. The third kitten was jet black apart from a white triangle on its chest and four white paws. They stared at her, their eyes huge in their skinny faces, their pointed ears standing upright.

'Here, little ones,' Mandy murmured, stopping and holding out her hand. 'I'm not going to hurt you.'

The black kitten ventured forward a few steps; he was still so young that his movements were unco-ordinated and his legs unsteady.

Mandy stayed still and waited. 'Come on,' she coaxed softly. 'It's OK.'

The black kitten wobbled closer. Very slowly, Mandy reached out and tickled him under his chin. He opened his mouth and mewed loudly.

Mandy smiled. He was absolutely adorable. Hearing his mew, the other two kittens began to come towards her. They were too young to have any real fear of humans and soon they were crowding round her as she stroked and tickled them.

Picking them up briefly, she checked underneath them and saw that the smaller grey-and-white one was a female, and the black one and the other grey-and-white one were males. The little female was shivering slightly and all three of them felt cold.

'They seem very friendly,' James said from the entrance to the passageway.

Mandy looked round. 'They are.' Reluctantly, she placed them back in their nest and backed out. 'But we've got to get them somewhere warm and dry.' She stroked Blackie, who was snuffling eagerly at the kitten smell on her jeans.

'Here's the mother,' Wilfred said softly, nodding to the yard entrance.

James immediately tightened his hold on Blackie's lead. Seeing them, the mother cat stopped in her tracks.

'It's all right,' Mandy said, crouching down. 'We won't hurt you.'

But the cat didn't seem to believe her. Turning on the spot, she fled back through the gate.

'Why's she so frightened?' James said, looking puzzled. 'I mean, she must have been tame when she belonged to Mr Oldfield.'

Wilfred rubbed his chin thoughtfully. 'Well, I'd say that judging by the size of her, she can't have been much more than a kitten when Arthur passed away. In which case, she'll have grown up without human contact.'

'So she's like a wild cat,' James said.

Wilfred nodded.

Mandy bit her lip thoughtfully. If the cat really was wild then it wasn't going to be easy to catch it. And it might even be a little dangerous. The poor thing might lash out if she was alarmed. 'We really should call Betty Hilder,' she said to James. 'She'll know what's best.'

'Is that the lady who runs the animal sanctuary on the other side of Welford?' asked Wilfred.

'That's right,' said Mandy. 'She often has stray cats to look after. She might be able to come and help us with this one.'

'Come into the house, then,' said Wilfred. He led the way into the old-fashioned kitchen with its big white sink and oak dresser.

The phone was by the window, and a local

telephone directory lay on the table beside it. James found the number for Welford Animal Sanctuary and read it out to Mandy.

She dialled the number, keeping her fingers crossed that Betty was in and could come out to Wilfred's place straight away. The sooner those kittens were taken somewhere warm and safe, the better.

'Welford Animal Sanctuary,' said a pleasant voice down the line.

That isn't Betty, Mandy thought, puzzled. 'Can I speak to Betty Hilder, please?' she asked.

'I'm sorry, Betty's on holiday,' came the reply. 'My name is Diana and I'm looking after the animals while she is away. Can I help you?'

Mandy thought rapidly. This lady sounded friendly, but would she be able to deal with a wild cat? 'My name is Mandy Hope,' she explained. 'I've found a stray cat and her three kittens, and I wanted to ask if Betty could come and collect them.'

'Oh, I don't think I can take any more animals while Betty isn't here,' Diana said apologetically. 'I'm rushed off my feet as it is. I'm really sorry but I just can't help you. Betty will be back next week – perhaps you could try her then.' Mandy heard a scuffle in the background. 'Oh no!' Diana exclaimed. 'One of Betty's dogs has just knocked the biscuit tin off the table. I'll have to go. Goodbye.' The phone went quiet.

Mandy's heart sank. Those kittens couldn't stay outside for another week! She noticed James looking anxiously at her.

'Betty's on holiday!' she told him in dismay. 'There's a lady called Diana looking after the animals, but she doesn't want to take in any more animals while Betty is away.'

'Would your parents be able to help?' asked James.

'They might, if they know Betty can't,' Mandy replied. She glanced at her watch. It was mid-morning; her parents would both be out on their rounds now. 'They won't be there at the moment though.'

'Well, come and see Matty first, then,' Wilfred offered. 'She'd like a visit.'

Mandy and James followed Wilfred out of the yard and through the gate that led into the campsite. The spaces where the tents had been pitched the summer before were now empty. But since they'd last visited, a number of old-fashioned wooden caravans had been added to the site, each freshly painted in a bright colour.

'I like the caravans,' James commented.

'Me too,' Mandy agreed. 'Though I'd have thought Sam Western would have gone for something really up-to-date,' she added. Sam Western was a local dairy farmer who owned a lot of land in the area. His farming methods were very modern and his barns were always filled with the latest machinery.

A smile caught at the corners of Wilfred's lips. 'Aye, I was surprised too,' he said. 'But then I spoke to the man delivering them, and he said that Mr Western had been offered them all as part of a business deal. He got them for a first-rate price apparently . . .'

'That explains it then.' James grinned. 'Sam Western never passes up an opportunity to make money.'

'Even if it's at the expense of animals,' Mandy said, her eyes darkening as she remembered the time that Sam Western had almost caused a herd of deer to be destroyed because he had wanted to cut down and sell the trees in the forest where they lived.

'Aye, he's certainly not over-fond of animals,' Wilfred agreed with her. 'It's lucky that cat didn't bring her kittens here. A few months ago, he found a couple of other cats living in the campsite shower block. I've never seen anyone so angry. He got rid of them straight away.'

'Got rid of them?' Mandy asked in alarm. 'How?'

'A man took them away,' Wilfred replied. 'Said he was going to "deal with them" for Mr Western. I didn't like the sound of it at all.'

Mandy shivered. She and James had had several run-ins with Sam Western in the past when he had tried to 'deal with' animals. 'Yes, thank goodness the grey cat came to you instead, Wilfred,' she agreed.

Wilfred nodded, then lifted his fingers to his lips. He whistled shrilly. They heard a distant whinny, and a few seconds later a silver grey mare came cantering over the hill towards them.

'Matty!' Mandy exclaimed in delight.

The grey mare stopped in front of them. She nuzzled Wilfred's gnarled hands before turning and giving Mandy and James a friendly sniff. Mandy took the apple she'd brought out of her pocket. 'Here, girl,' she said, offering it from her open palm.

'She'll be glad when the campsite opens again at Easter, won't you, girl?' Wilfred said, as Matty crunched happily on the apple. 'She's been getting bored with nothing to do.'

Smiling, Mandy nodded. When the campsite was open, Matty gave rides to the children who stayed there. They loved her.

'But I'm going to have to get her fit again first,' Wilfred went on. 'I haven't ridden her much over the winter, my back's been playing me up.' An idea suddenly seemed to strike him. 'I don't suppose you two would be able to give me a hand getting her fit again, would you? If you like, you could take her out for a few rides.'

'Oh, yes!' Mandy gasped, her eyes shining.

'Definitely!' James agreed. Though he wasn't quite as keen on riding as Mandy, he loved riding gentle old Matty. 'We're on half-term all week so we could come up each day, Wilfred.'

Wilfred smiled. 'Well, that would be grand.'

Mandy hugged the gentle mare. 'Oh, Matty!'

she said. 'Did you hear that? We're going to have such fun!'

Two

'I hope Mum or Dad's here,' Mandy said, as she and James cycled into the Animal Ark driveway later that morning.

Simon, Animal Ark's young veterinary nurse, was stocking up with boxes of wormers behind the reception desk. 'Hi,' he said cheerfully as they entered.

'Are Mum and Dad back, Simon?' Mandy asked.

'Nope, they're both still out,' Simon replied. 'Your mum rang to say she'd been held up at Grove Farm, but your dad should be here soon.'

Then, seeing Mandy's face fall, he added, 'What's up? Can I help?'

'I don't know,' Mandy sighed. She explained about the grey cat and her kittens, and the fact that Betty Hilder couldn't help because she was on holiday.

Simon looked concerned. 'Kittens are very vulnerable to disease at such a young age. They need to be put somewhere warm as quickly as possible.'

'Mmm, that's what we thought,' Mandy said, even more worried now Simon had confirmed her fears for the kittens.

Just then, the door opened and Adam Hope came into the surgery wearing his farm clothes: green padded jacket, thick trousers and wellingtons. In one hand he carried a cardboard box. His blue eyes took in the little group by the reception desk. 'What's all this then?' he asked. 'You three look as thick as thieves.'

'Dad!' Mandy exclaimed. 'There's a stray cat up at Wilfred's with three kittens!' She quickly repeated the story. '. . . And as Betty can't help, we *have* to, Dad!' she finished.

Mr Hope thought for a few seconds, then

nodded. 'I think we should go up there early tomorrow, before morning surgery,' he decided.

Simon nodded. 'You can count me in, too.'

'And me,' said James.

'Thanks, Dad!' Mandy cried. She gave her father a hug. 'But how are we going to catch the mother?' she asked worriedly. 'We have to persuade her that we don't want to hurt her or her kittens.'

'Could we tame her by leaving food out for her?' James suggested. 'That's what we did with Blossom.' Blossom was another stray cat turned feral whom they had once helped.

Mr Hope rubbed his beard. 'I think we need a faster solution, James,' he replied. 'If the kittens are cold then the sooner we can get them inside the better.'

'And there's always the danger that the mother might feel threatened by attempts to tame her and decide to move the kittens somewhere else,' Simon added.

Adam Hope nodded. 'If enough of us go, we should be able to corner her. We can win her trust later, when she and her kittens are safe.' Then he looked at his watch. 'Well, now that's sorted out, how about we have some lunch?' he said, holding up a cardboard box. 'You'll stay won't you, James? I can offer you handbaked vegetable pasties straight from Sam Western's new organic farm!'

'Sam Western's got an organic farm?' Mandy said in surprise. 'Since when?'

'He's owned it for a couple of months,' her dad replied. 'He doesn't run it himself – he has a tenant farmer. But I think he saw that there was money to be made in organic produce. The farm shop certainly charged me enough for these pasties. Still, they look delicious.'

Mandy grinned and patted her father's rather portly stomach. 'You think all food looks delicious!'

'I shall ignore that comment,' her dad said with mock dignity. 'Now, who wants some lunch?'

The pasties *were* delicious. After lunch, Mandy and James helped clear the plates away and then cycled back to Wilfred's. They took with them a piece of sheepskin bedding and more newspaper for the kittens, and some build-up formula cat food for the mother. But when they knocked on Wilfred's door, there was no answer.

'He must have gone out,' James said. 'Let's take

the stuff round to the backyard for the cat.'

'At least the sheepskin should keep the kittens warm tonight,' Mandy commented as they walked into the yard.

The mother cat was prowling around by the entrance to the passageway when they arrived, but as soon as she saw them she flattened her ears and shot away.

'She's so skinny,' James said, watching her streak across the road.

'It can't have been easy for her trying to feed three kittens and catch food for herself,' Mandy said, her heart going out to the young creature.

While James hung on to Blackie, Mandy edged down the passageway with the sheepskin. The kittens seemed pleased to see her. As she crouched down to say hello, they tumbled out of their newspaper nest and walked unsteadily towards her, mewing.

Mandy stroked each of them in turn. The adventurous black kitten began to pat at the laces on her trainers with one tiny front paw. However, he didn't quite have the balance to stand on three legs and he tumbled over in a small furry heap. Mandy laughed and scooped him up into her

arms. 'You are a little pickle,' she said, kissing him on his nose. He stared at her for a moment with his big blue eyes and then miaowed loudly.

Although Mandy could have happily sat there and played with the kittens for hours, she knew she had work to do. Putting the black kitten down, she set about clearing away the soiled and damp newspaper and then laid down the piece of sheepskin bedding, with more clean newspaper on top. 'It's only for one more night,' she promised the kittens. 'Tomorrow we'll take you somewhere safe and dry.' Then she scooped up the dirty newspaper, carried it out of the passageway, and put it into Wilfred's bin.

'Now we'll just leave the mother's food out nearby,' James said. 'And hopefully she'll find it when she comes back.'

When everything was done, Mandy wrote a note for Wilfred saying they would be back early the next morning and then cycled back with James to Animal Ark.

They arrived just as afternoon surgery was starting and the waiting-room was filling up with patients. Several people were lined up at the desk talking to Jean Knox, the grey-haired receptionist. Eager to say hello to everyone, Blackie lunged forwards, his tongue hanging out, and tail wagging

'I'd better take him home,' James said, struggling to hang on to the excitable Labrador. 'What time should I come round tomorrow?'

'Meet here at six-thirty, so Mum and Dad can come with us before morning surgery,' Mandy said.

'Six-thirty!' James groaned. 'That's so early!'

'Of course, you don't have to come—' Mandy began.

'No, no. I'll be here,' James said hastily.

Mandy grinned. She'd known that, despite his moaning, James wouldn't miss the morning's adventure for anything. 'See you then,' she said.

As James left, Mandy hurried through to the office and slipped on her white coat. She loved helping in the surgery. There were lots of things to do – helping to hold and comfort patients, fetching medicines for her mum and dad, wiping down the examination tables with disinfectant – not to mention mopping up puddles on the floor . . .

Although Mandy was busy, she found time to pop into the residential unit to see how Dylan was. The puppy was still lying quietly in his cage without moving. Mandy checked his water and stroked him for a little while before going back into the surgery.

Just as she came out of the residential unit, her mum appeared at the door of one of the examination rooms. 'Hello, love,' she said. 'Have you got a moment? Simon's in with Dad and I could use an extra pair of hands.'

'Sure,' Mandy said eagerly. She followed her mum into the examination room. A woman and a young girl were standing next to the examination table. On top of it was a rabbit carrier.

'I need to put some eye-drops in,' Mrs Hope explained. 'If you could just help to hold him, Mandy. He's being a bit lively.'

Mandy nodded and watched her mum flip open the lid of the carrier.

The cream-coloured rabbit inside struggled wildly in Emily Hope's arms when she took him out. But, gradually, he began to calm down a little.

'Fluffy's got sore eyes,' the little girl told Mandy.

'That's right,' Mrs Hope said, smiling at her. 'It's called conjunctivitis. But these drops should soon make him feel better.' She gave the rabbit to Mandy to hold.

He bucked a little, but Mandy knew how to hold on firmly but gently. She watched her mum squeeze the drops into Fluffy's eyes. He blinked but kept calm in Mandy's arms. 'All done,' she told him gently, and then she put him back in his carrier.

Mrs Hope explained about the medicine that Fluffy needed to the girl's mother and then she showed them out of the examination room, leaving Mandy to wipe over the table.

'Archie Austin,' Mandy heard her mum call into the waiting-room.

A moment later, her mum reappeared with an elderly woman leading a brown-and-white springer spaniel. He was walking slowly and the dark hair round his muzzle was heavily flecked with grey.

'So what's wrong with Archie, Mrs Austin?' Mrs Hope asked, shutting the door.

Mrs Austin looked worried. 'Well, he's been limping on his front left leg for a while,' she began. 'I thought it was just arthritis because he's sixteen years old now, but it seems to be getting worse.'

Mrs Hope lifted Archie on to the consulting table and began to run her hands over his legs. 'There is a bit of a lump here,' she said, her experienced fingers probing Archie's left leg above his wrist. 'Have you noticed any other changes in his behaviour?'

'Well, he's been ever so quiet over the last few weeks and he's also been off his food,' Mrs Austin replied. 'I know he's old but he's always been so healthy until now.'

Mrs Hope nodded. 'OK, I'll just give him a

general check over. Mandy, can you hold his head, please?'

Mandy moved up to the table and gently but firmly took hold of Archie on either side of his head. 'Good boy,' she told him. He looked up at her with deep, trusting eyes while her mum checked his glands, looked in his mouth, listened to his heart and took his temperature.

Finally, Mrs Hope straightened up and rubbed Archie's head. 'I think I'm going to need to X-ray him, Mrs Austin,' she said. 'The lameness could just be the result of a knock or arthritis but I need to check that it's nothing more serious. At his age, we can't rule out the possibility of a bone tumour.'

Mrs Austin swallowed. 'If anything happened to Archie, I don't know what I'd do,' she said, her voice shaking slightly. 'Since my husband died last year, he's been my best friend.'

Seeing Mrs Austin's distress, Mandy felt awful. She stroked Archie's ears and the little spaniel licked her hand.

Mrs Hope looked at Mrs Austin sympathetically. 'Please try not to worry too much,' she said. 'Like I said, it may well be nothing serious.' She turned to the computer on the side table and studied the bookings for the next few days. 'We can X-ray him on Wednesday morning, if that's all right for you?'

Mrs Austin nodded.

'Bring him in at eight-thirty in the morning,' Mrs Hope said. 'You'll be able to collect him that afternoon but he'll be a bit wobbly from the anaesthetic. Have you got someone who can give you a lift?'

Mrs Austin nodded. 'My son. He brought me in today.'

'Good,' Mrs Hope said. She patted Archie. 'Well, we'll see you then. Mandy, can you show Mrs Austin out?'

Mandy nodded and held the door open for Mrs Austin and Archie. Despite her mum's words, Mrs Austin's face was lined with worry. Mandy felt her heart twist as she watched the spaniel walking stiffly beside his owner. It was horrible seeing animals get old. 'Bye, Archie,' she said softly. 'See you on Wednesday.'

When surgery finished, Mandy helped Simon to mop the floors and clean the surfaces ready for the next day, and then she went through to the residential unit to see Dylan.

The puppy still lay on his stomach, his ears flopping sadly. Mandy kneeled down beside him and stroked his head. 'Poor boy,' she said. 'You still don't look very happy.'

Just then, the door opened and Simon came in. 'How is he?' he asked.

'Just the same,' Mandy replied. 'Is he paralysed, Simon?' She had seen cats and dogs after road accidents who had sustained such injuries to their spine that their legs would no longer work, and she wondered if that would be the case with Dylan.

'No,' Simon said. He picked up one of Dylan's big white paws. 'His pads are warm and look . . .' He pinched the skin between Dylan's toes. After a few seconds the puppy moved his foot away. 'His reflexes are slower than normal but he can still react to pain. If he was paralysed he wouldn't be able to move his paw at all.'

Mandy sighed in relief.

Then Simon put his hands under the puppy and gently tried to lift him into a standing position. But Dylan's legs refused to carry his weight, and Simon let the puppy flop back down. 'He should be ready to stand and move by now, though,' Simon observed, frowning. 'He's going to have to show some more progress soon in order to have chance of a full recovery. If not, your mum and dad might advise that it would be kindest to put him down . . .'

Mandy gasped in shock. She looked at the pup's sad face. He looked really depressed. 'Have his owners been to see him yet?' she asked.

Simon shook his head. 'Your dad advised them not to come in until Dylan had recovered a little, in case he got too excited.' Simon replied. 'But they've already rung three times today to see how he is – they're obviously really worried.'

Mandy looked at the puppy. 'Maybe he's just missing them. It must be really strange for him being away from his home.'

Simon patted Dylan. 'Maybe.' He stood up. 'Well, I'd better get going. I'll see you tomorrow, about six-thirty, for a spot of cat catching.'

'Yeah, see you then,' Mandy replied.

The door shut behind Simon and Mandy was left on her own with Dylan. She sat stroking him for a long time.

* * *

Mandy's alarm clock woke her up at a quarter to six the next morning. It was still dark outside and she could hear a light rain pattering on her window. Her heart sank – the kittens! The sooner they got them warm and dry the better. She threw back the covers and leaped out of bed.

Her mum was already in the kitchen, filling the kettle to make coffee. 'Have you got everything we need for catching these cats?' she asked. Mrs Hope had volunteered to help, too.

Mandy nodded. The night before she had got out two cat carriers, some food, a bowl, several thick blankets and five pairs of sturdy gloves. The plan was to put down the food and then to catch the mother cat while she was eating, throwing a blanket over her so that she couldn't scratch them or escape. With five pairs of hands, they hoped they could block all the escape routes. Mandy knew that the cat would be frightened, but as she looked at the rain falling outside she knew that they had to do it. If the weather worsened, then the kittens might not survive.

At six-thirty, everyone assembled in the waiting-room in warm coats and scarves.

James came in last, yawning loudly and looking bleary-eyed. 'I can't believe I've got up this early,' he grumbled as they all climbed into the Hopes' Land-rover.

'Just think of the cat and her kittens,' Mandy said, handing him a carrier to hold.

'Now, we'll need to be quiet when we get there,' Adam Hope warned them. 'We don't want the mother taking fright and running off. Mandy, I suggest that you go into the yard and leave the food near the entrance to the passageway. Simon, you and James block off the yard gate. Emily and I will stay near the back of the yard and move in once the cat is eating.'

Dawn was just breaking as they reached Wilfred's cottage. Emily Hope handed out the gloves and then they all got quietly out of the Land-rover. The rain had stopped and the air seemed still and quiet. No one said a word.

Mandy took the bowl of food and cautiously opened the gate. It creaked slightly. The noise seemed very loud and Mandy froze for a moment, holding her breath. But nothing happened. After a few seconds, she began to breathe again. She crept forward, her eyes adjusting to the dim light.

As she crossed the yard, she could hear the faint sounds of the others moving into position behind her.

She reached the entrance to the passageway. Putting down the food bowl, she peered into the darkness. The white sheepskin bedding was just visible at the end. Mandy stared. The nest was deserted.

The cat and her kittens had gone!

Three

Mandy looked round. 'They're not here!' she called out. The others came forward, looking surprised.

'The mother cat must have moved them,' her mum groaned, looking down the passageway. 'I guess all the activity yesterday must have been too much for her. Feral cats do sometimes move their young to a new nest if they feel threatened.'

Mandy stared at her. 'So she moved them because of us?'

Her mum put an arm round her shoulders. 'Don't blame yourself, you were only trying to help.'

'What will happen to the kittens?' James asked. His voice was shaky and Mandy was sure that, despite her mum's comforting words, he felt as bad as she did. It was awful to think the cat had moved her family because of their interference.

'It all depends where they've gone,' Mrs Hope said. 'If it's somewhere safe and dry then they'll be OK.'

'They might not have gone far,' Simon said hopefully. 'We could look for them.'

'I guess it's worth a try,' Mr Hope agreed.

They set about searching the rest of the yard and the hedgerows outside.

They had been looking for ten minutes when Wilfred came out of his house. 'What's going on?' he asked, looking at the search party in surprise.

Feeling terrible, Mandy explained.

Wilfred's face fell. 'Poor little mites,' he said. 'They were there when I went to bed last night. I went out to check on them. Here, I'll get my coat and help you look. There's a copse of trees down the road, maybe they've gone there.'

He went into the house and reappeared a minute later, wearing a heavy coat, then led the way to the little wood.

'We have to find them,' Mandy said desperately to James. She kept imagining the kittens huddling together, cold and damp, on a bed of leaves.

James nodded, his eyes anxious behind his glasses. 'The weather's supposed to get colder tonight. I heard it on the TV. They were saying that there might be a frost.'

Feeling worse than ever, Mandy began to search. She looked under bushes, in hollow tree-trunks, in piles of leaves – but there was no sign of the kittens.

At quarter to eight, Mr and Mrs Hope shook their heads. 'We're going to have to stop looking,' Emily Hope said.

'We can't!' Mandy protested.

'We have to, love,' said her mum. 'Dad and I have got to prepare for morning surgery.'

'I'm sorry, Mandy, but I'll have to stop as well,' said Wilfred. 'Matty will be wondering where her breakfast is!'

'Well, we'll stay and keep looking,' James said, looking at Mandy. 'There's loads more places to check – there's the campsite for a start.'

'You must be very careful if you see these cats,' Adam Hope warned. 'The mother cat might panic if you try to catch her and she'll scratch and bite if she thinks her kittens are in danger. Try to get her used to you by giving her some food. Then she might let you pick her up, but don't forget to wear the gloves!'

'OK, Dad, we'll be really careful,' Mandy promised. 'Come on, James, let's get going!'

'Oh – and what about breakfast? You haven't eaten yet,' Mrs Hope suddenly remembered.

'Breakfast!' Mandy echoed. She couldn't even think about food with the kittens missing.

'Tell you what,' Wilfred said suddenly. 'I can rustle up a few sandwiches for these two later on, no problem.'

'Oh, yes please!' Mandy said, looking pleadingly at her mum.

'OK,' Mrs Hope agreed. 'I'll ring your house, James, and let your parents know what's happening. But don't get your hopes up too high. The cat could have gone anywhere.'

After waving Mr and Mrs Hope and Simon off, Mandy and James hurried to the campsite. 'I don't know whether I want the cat to be here or not,' James panted as they ran across the field to the shower block. 'You know what Wilfred said yesterday about Sam Western getting rid of those cats.'

Mandy remembered only too well. 'If she is here we'll just have to move her before he finds out,' she said firmly.

They searched every inch of the shower block. Behind the wooden partition at one end, they could hear Matty shifting in the straw.

'Let's try Matty's stable and feed store,' Mandy said.

Matty greeted Mandy and James with a soft whicker. Mandy went up and stroked her velvety grey nose. However, it didn't take long to see that Matty was the only animal in the stable area. There was no sign of the cat or her kittens.

'Let's go and check under the caravans,' James said.

They were just leaving the stable block when Wilfred appeared with a Thermos flask of tea and some sandwiches. 'Any sign of the kittens?' he asked.

'No,' Mandy replied. 'We're going to look round the caravans.'

'Well, you want to be quick,' Wilfred said. 'Sam Western's coming up here some time today. I think he's planning on getting the campsite ready to open again. You don't want him to catch sight of the cat if she's here.'

'No, we don't,' Mandy said in alarm. 'Come on, James!'

They ran over to the caravans and checked quickly underneath them.

'Nothing,' James said at last, as they walked unhappily back to the stable block.

Wilfred had brought Matty out and was tying her up outside so that he could clean her stall. 'Cup of tea?' he offered, looking at their faces.

Mandy and James shook their heads.

'Now don't you fret,' Wilfred said kindly. 'That cat's been living in the wild for some time now. She'll know how to look after herself. Why don't you take a break from all this searching and give me a hand with Matty? You ought to have something to eat too.'

Mandy looked at James. She didn't want to give up looking for the cat but where else was there to look? They seemed to have searched everywhere.

James shrugged. 'OK,' he said to Wilfred.

'Grand,' Wilfred said. 'She could do with a brush over.'

After finishing the sandwiches, Mandy and James fetched the grooming kit from the feed store and set to work. As Mandy brushed Matty's face, the mare nuzzled her gently. It was as if she could sense Mandy's distress.

'What are we going to do?' James said.

'I don't know,' Mandy replied. 'We've got to find her.' She moved round to brush Matty's tail and suddenly gasped. Running across the field was the grey cat. 'James!' she cried. 'Look!'

But by the time James had turned, the cat had disappeared through the hedge. 'What am I looking at?' he asked, confused.

'It was the cat!' Mandy exclaimed. 'Come on!' Throwing down the grooming brush she was using, she set off across the field.

'Are you sure?' James panted as they ran through the long grass.

'Positive,' Mandy said. They reached the hedge. 'She must have got through here.' Bending down, she pointed out a gap just large enough for the cat to have squeezed through.

James looked over to the other side of the hedge, where a field stretched out. 'She could be anywhere,' he said, looking round the empty open space.

Mandy knew he was right. 'At least we know she's somewhere nearby,' she said, thinking fast. 'We'll have to keep watch for when she comes through here again. Then, when she does, we can follow her to the kittens.'

James nodded, fixing his glasses more firmly on his nose. 'And let's leave some food out for her nearby,' he suggested.

'Good idea,' Mandy agreed.

They hurried back to Wilfred's cottage and fetched the bowl of food they'd brought from Animal Ark.

'Sam Western's not going to like this,' James said, as they placed the bowl near the hedge.

'So we mustn't let him find out,' Mandy said. 'Luckily the caravans are nowhere near here so he might not even come this way.' But just to be on the safe side she arranged some long grass round the bowl so that it couldn't be seen from a distance. 'Now all we need to do is to watch it,' she said.

'We could carry on grooming Matty while we wait,' James suggested.

They went back up to Matty and finished brushing her, all the time keeping one eye on the hole in the hedge and the feed bowl nearby.

At last, Matty's grey coat was clean and her mane and tail were silky and tangle-free.

Wilfred came out of the stable block. He smiled at Mandy and James. 'You've done a good job there,' he remarked.

'We've enjoyed it,' Mandy said, and she meant it. Ever since she had caught that fleeting glimpse of the cat, she had been feeling much happier. She was sure that they would find the kittens now. It was just a case of waiting.

'Now how about riding Matty for me?' Wilfred suggested.

Mandy looked at James.

'We might as well,' he said. 'We can still watch out for the cat and, anyway, it might be ages before she comes back.'

They fetched Matty's tack from the storeroom and each picked a riding-hat from the store that Wilfred kept for the campers to use.

'Just take it gently,' Wilfred said, as Mandy pulled down the stirrup and prepared to mount. 'I've got some tidying to do in the house so I'll leave you to it. When you've finished, give her a rub down and turn her loose.'

Mandy nodded, then swung herself into the saddle. It felt wonderful to be on Matty again. 'If you keep watch while I ride,' she said to James, 'then we can swap.'

'OK,' he agreed.

Mandy rode Matty down the field. The obedient mare walked, trotted and cantered exactly when Mandy asked. 'You're such a lovely old girl, Matty,' Mandy told her, patting her smooth neck. And Matty tossed her head as if she understood.

Half an hour later, Mandy and James untacked Matty and rubbed her down.

'That was fun,' Mandy said, smiling happily as they turned Matty loose in the field. The mare immediately put her head down and started to graze.

'Still no sign of the cat though,' James said, glancing towards the bowl. 'Hey!' he said, grabbing Mandy's arm. 'Look!'

Mandy swung round. It was the cat! Crouching nervously by the food bowl, she was eating great, hungry mouthfuls. 'Quick!' Mandy exclaimed.

They began to hurry round the outside of the field. As they drew nearer, James slowed down. 'We mustn't upset her,' he hissed to Mandy. 'We don't want her running away again.'

Mandy nodded and they began to creep towards the cat as quietly as they could. *If we can just get near enough to follow her* . . . Mandy thought. She could feel her heart beating quickly in her chest. The cat mustn't escape from them again.

Just then, the cat finished the food and looked up. Mandy and James froze but the cat didn't seem to notice them. With a shake of her head, she began trotting purposefully up the field.

'Where's she going?' Mandy whispered, in surprise. She had expected the cat to go back through the hedge.

'I don't know,' replied James. 'Let's follow her.'

Keeping a safe distance, they began to run quietly after the thin grey shape.

'She's heading for the caravans,' Mandy said suddenly.

Veering to the left, the cat made a beeline for the caravan furthest away from the campsite entrance. Reaching it, she trotted round the back.

A moment later, Mandy and James stopped beside the bright orange caravan. They looked all round but the cat had vanished.

'Look!' James whispered, pointing at the side of the caravan. One of the planks of wood had come loose and there was a gap just big enough for a cat to squeeze through. 'Maybe she's inside.'

Very cautiously, they stole across the grass to

the caravan window. It was high up, but by standing on the wheel, Mandy could just see inside. Her heart leaped. 'She's in there!' she whispered excitedly to James.

The cat was standing in the middle of the caravan and her kittens were stumbling round her. Mandy got down so that James could climb on to the wheel and have a look too. 'They're all there,' he said, breathing out in relief.

Suddenly a horrible thought struck Mandy. 'But what about Sam Western?' she gasped. 'Remember he's coming to check out the caravans today. If he finds the kittens . . .' Her voice trailed off as she stared at James.

The relief drained from his face. 'You know what Wilfred said happened to those other cats,' James said slowly. He jumped off the wheel on to the ground.

'We can't let Sam Western find them here, James!' Mandy exclaimed.

'But what can we do?' he said in dismay. 'We can't get into the caravan.'

Mandy looked at the shut window and the locked door. James was right. There was no way in apart from through the gap in the side and that was far too small for a person to get through. For a moment, Mandy thought wildly about breaking the window, but even if they did that, how would they get the cat out? She was so scared of humans that it was going to be very difficult to catch her. Mandy made a decision. 'Let's go and ring Mum and Dad from Wilfred's house,' she said. 'See what they say.'

'But what if the cat's heard us?' James said. 'What if she moves the kittens while we're gone? Or what if Sam Western comes?'

Mandy hadn't thought of that. She bit her lip anxiously.

'Look, I'll stay and keep watch. You go,' James said, looking determined. 'But be quick!'

'OK!' Mandy gasped. She set off across the field as fast as she could go. By the time she reached Wilfred's door, her heart was pounding and her breath was coming in short gasps. Panting loudly, she banged the knocker hard. *Please hurry, Wilfred!* she thought.

Wilfred opened the door. His eyes took in her frantic face. 'Whatever's the matter, lass?' he demanded.

'The cats – they're in one of the caravans–'

Gradually, Mandy found enough breath to gasp out the whole story. 'Can I use your phone, Wilfred?' she finished. 'I want to ring Mum and Dad.'

'Of course,' Wilfred said. 'You know where it is.'

Mandy hurried through the kitchen to the phone. Grabbing the receiver, she dialled the Animal Ark number.

Jean Knox answered almost at once, but to Mandy's dismay she couldn't help. 'I'm sorry, Mandy love,' Jean said, 'but your dad's out on his rounds and your mum's in the operating theatre with Simon. I can give her a message when she's finished.'

'Can you tell her that we've found the cat and her kittens, please?' Mandy said desperately. 'But they're in one of the caravans and Sam Western's coming. We don't know what to do.'

'I'll tell her,' Jean promised.

Mandy put the phone down, feeling frustrated and helpless.

'Now, now, lass,' said Wilfred sympathetically. 'Don't you go getting so upset. We'll get those cats out. You just go and fetch the stuff you brought this morning.'

'But how will we get into the caravan?' Mandy asked.

Wilfred tapped his nose. 'Leave that to me.'

A ray of hope suddenly lightened Mandy's despair. If Wilfred could open the caravan then maybe she and James *would* be able to get the cats out by themselves. She raced outside and picked up the cat food and gloves that her mum and dad had left.

Soon, she and Wilfred were hurrying down the field. In one hand, Wilfred swung a metal bar which was flattened at one end. 'This should be just what we need,' he'd said as he produced it from his old wooden toolbox in the hall.

As they neared the orange caravan, Mandy broke into a run.

'I thought you were never coming back!' James exclaimed. His face was anxious. 'Did you speak to your mum and dad?'

Mandy shook her head. 'I couldn't. They were both busy. But Wilfred's going to help. He thinks he can open the caravan door.' She dumped the carriers, gloves, blankets and food on the grass. 'We're going to have to catch the cat ourselves.'

James looked thoughtful. 'Before we go in, we should block off the loose plank so that the cat can't escape that way,' he said quickly. 'Let's get a bale of hay.'

Mandy only just stopped herself from hugging him. That was the best thing about James; when there was an animal in trouble he never stopped thinking of ways to help it.

Leaving Wilfred to examine the door, Mandy and James fetched a bale of hay from the stable block. They struggled back across the grass with it and wedged it against the side of the caravan so that it blocked off the loose plank.

'Right, I think I can get this door open,' Wilfred said, looking at them.

Mandy remembered her dad telling her that if the cat was frightened then she would scratch and bite. She handed James a pair of gloves. 'We'd better put these on,' she said.

'What did your mum and dad say this morning about catching them?' James asked.

'Well, we want to try and keep her as calm as possible,' Mandy said. 'If she panics she'll be impossible to catch. One of us should go in and put some food on the floor. Then, as she's eating, we'll try and pick her up and get her into a carrier.' Mandy bit her lip. She knew that the cat would hate being confined in the carrier but if they were going to help her then it was the only thing to do. She hoped that once they had the cat in a safe place they could teach her that humans were kind and not to be feared.

James nodded and picked up the food.

'Are you ready?' Wilfred asked.

Mandy took a deep breath and picked up the carriers. 'We're ready,' she said.

Wilfred picked up the metal bar.

'Hey!' An irate voice rang out behind them.

Mandy swung round. A smart black Land-rover had drawn into the campsite. The driver's door was open and a stocky, fair-haired man wearing a green waxed jacket was striding towards them. His face was red with anger.

'Sam Western!' Mandy gasped to James.

Four

'Just what do you think you are doing?' Sam Western demanded furiously. As he reached the caravan, his thunderous blue eyes took in Mandy and James. 'You two!' he exclaimed. 'What are you troublemakers doing here?' He glared at Wilfred. 'And what are you doing with my caravan?'

Wilfred looked like he didn't know what to say. He flushed to the roots of his white hair. 'Well, er, it's like this, Mr Western,' he began.

'It's our fault,' Mandy broke in quickly. She didn't want Wilfred to get into trouble. If Sam

Western wanted to, he could order Wilfred to take Matty off the campsite.

'We asked Wilfred to help us,' James said, backing Mandy up.

'Help you do what?' Sam Western exploded. 'Break into one of my caravans?'

'We had to!' Mandy burst out. 'There's a cat inside!'

For a moment there was silence. Sam Western stared at her as if he couldn't believe what she was saying. 'There's a *what*?' he said, speaking very slowly.

'A cat,' James said. 'And her kittens. We were trying to get them out.'

'Cats!' Sam Western's face creased with a look of repulsion. 'We'll soon see about that!' He pulled a bunch of keys from his pocket and, pushing Mandy and James out of the way, strode to the caravan door.

Mandy leaped after him. 'Please don't frighten them,' she gasped. 'The kittens are only tiny and the cat will panic.'

'Mr Western,' Wilfred put in, 'please be reasonable . . .'

But Sam Western ignored them. Turning the

key in the lock, he wrenched open the door and marched up the steps.

'Quick, James!' Mandy cried. 'Get ready to catch them if they come out!'

As they leaped towards the open door, they heard Sam Western shout, 'Right! Come here, you!'

They heard a hiss and a yowl – and then Sam Western started yelling.

Mandy's hands flew to her mouth. What was going on?

The next instant, Sam Western came staggering backwards out of the caravan. One hand was clutching the other. 'It attacked me!' he cried, blood oozing from his injured hand.

Mandy stood rooted to the spot in shock but James, showing great presence of mind, darted up the steps and slammed the door shut. 'Now they can't escape!' he gasped to Mandy.

'Escape!' Sam Western echoed. 'You're worried about the cat? It just attacked me!'

'Well, what did you expect?' Mandy cried. 'She thought you were trying to take her kittens! She was just defending them.'

'Defending them!' Sam Western spat. 'We'll

soon see about that.' Shaking with rage, he turned and stormed towards his Land-rover.

Mandy felt a cold shiver of fear run down her spine. She raced after him. 'What are you going to do?' she gasped.

'I'm going to get my hand seen to, then I'm going to get someone to deal with those cats,' Sam Western told her grimly.

'What do you mean?' Mandy cried in alarm.

But Sam Western didn't answer her. He had reached his Land-rover and he jumped in.

'Please, Mr Western!' Mandy exclaimed, grabbing the door before he could shut it. 'We'll move them for you. We'll take them away.' Her mind raced. 'And it won't waste your men's time!'

Sam Western glared at her. The deep scratch marks stood out vividly on his left hand but the mention of saving time seemed to have got his attention. 'You've got until lunch-time,' he snapped. 'If they're not gone by one o'clock, I'm getting someone in to do it.'

He slammed the door shut and then drove off, revving the Land-rover's powerful engine noisily as he sped across the grass.

James came running up to Mandy. 'What's happening?' he demanded.

Mandy turned round, her face pale. 'We've got until one o'clock to move the cats. Come on!'

Although both Mandy and James wanted to get straight back into the caravan and catch the cats, they knew they had to be patient. The mother cat was going to be terrified after her encounter with Sam Western and so they decided to give the cat half an hour to calm down. To help pass the time, they cleaned Matty's saddle and bridle for Wilfred.

'What are we going to do if we can't catch the mother cat?' James said, as they rubbed damp sponges over the leather.

Mandy didn't even want to think about what would happen. 'We'll get her out,' she said, jutting out her chin in determination.

Just as they were finishing the tack, a white van drove into the campsite. A group of workmen jumped out and began unloading some tools from the van.

'Take them over to the ditches,' a sharp-faced man directed them. Mandy immediately recognised him as Dennis Saville, Sam Western's hard-hearted estate manager.

'They must be Sam Western's men come to sort out the campsite,' she said, as the men started to carry the tools across the field.

'I hope they don't upset Matty,' James said, watching the grey mare skitter out of the men's way.

Just then, Dennis Saville caught sight of them. He strode over. 'What are you two doing here?' he demanded, his humourless features creasing into a frown. 'This is private property.'

'We're helping Wilfred,' James said, holding up the bridle he had just finished putting back together.

'And we're trying to get a cat out of one of the caravans for Mr Western,' Mandy added, forcing herself to be polite. She didn't want Dennis Saville interfering. 'She's living there with her kittens.'

Dennis Saville's eyebrows rose. 'A cat!' he said incredulously. 'Oh-ho, the boss won't like that.'

'He didn't,' James muttered under his breath.

'Well, we're going to move her,' Mandy continued bravely. 'Then Mr Western won't have to see her again.'

'A stray, is she?' Dennis Saville said.

Mandy and James nodded.

The estate manager gave a short laugh. 'I might have known. You two are always running round the countryside interfering with things. Rescuing foxes one minute. Stray cats the next. If it was up to me, I'd get the boss's dogs and flush her out.'

Mandy's temper snapped and she jumped to her feet. 'Well it's not up to you!' she exclaimed. 'Mr Western told us we could have until one o'clock to move her, so you'd better just leave her alone!'

Dennis Saville stepped towards her. 'Or what?' he said menacingly.

James grabbed Mandy's arm. 'We're only trying to help,' he said quickly to Dennis Saville before Mandy could reply. 'We'll move the cat.'

'You'd better,' Dennis Saville said. 'Or I'll do it for you.' He turned on his heel and strode away.

Infuriated beyond belief, Mandy struggled to get away from James but he hung on to her. 'Calm down!' he urged. 'It won't do the cats any good.'

Mandy quickly realised that James was right. If they antagonised Dennis Saville then maybe he would carry out his threat and fetch Sam Western's fierce bulldogs. She took a deep breath. 'OK.'

'Come on,' James said. 'Let's go and see if we can get that cat out.'

Putting the saddle and bridle away, they went to the caravan. At the side of the field, the men were shouting to each other as they began to clear out the ditches. Mandy listened at the caravan door. It was quiet inside. 'OK,' she said, her heart beating fast. 'Let's go in.'

She pushed open the door just a crack, her hands ready to slam it shut if the cat tried to escape. She waited for the cat to yowl and leap. But nothing happened. Mandy put her eye to the crack. At first it was too dark to see anything, but gradually her eyes adapted to the dim light. 'I can see her,' she whispered to James. 'She's with the kittens at the back.'

As quietly as she could, Mandy pushed the door open and slipped inside. James followed her, carrying the bowl of food, and quickly shut the door behind him. The air smelled strongly of cats. The only light filtered in through a chink in the curtains.

At the far end of the caravan the mother cat

had risen to her feet and was staring at them, her skinny grey back arched and the hair on her spine standing up. Her kittens were sleeping beside her on an old newspaper. Opening her mouth, she drew her lips back and hissed warningly.

James pushed the bowl of food as far as he could towards her.

'Let's sit down,' Mandy whispered. 'It'll make us seem less threatening.'

They crouched down by the door. As the minutes ticked by, the hair on the cat's back gradually flattened but she didn't move. She stood over her kittens, her muscles tense, watching them with her large amber eyes.

'It's OK,' Mandy murmured. 'We won't hurt you.' Wondering if she could get closer, she began to inch across the floor. The cat's hair immediately rose again and she spat loudly.

Mandy quickly moved back. The spitting sound woke the black kitten. Blinking sleepily, he saw Mandy and James and began to amble towards them. With one swift movement, the mother cat shot out her front paw and cuffed him soundly. He rolled over with a startled miaow. Scrambling to his feet, he stumbled back to the newspaper and curled up beside his brother and sister.

'Poor thing!' Mandy whispered in distress.

'The mother's never going to let us anywhere near her,' James whispered back. 'She's not even looking at the food.'

'She will,' Mandy said optimistically. 'She'll get used to us in the end.'

But after an hour had passed and the cat had shown no sign of relaxing with them, even Mandy's spirits started to fall.

'Come on,' James sighed. 'This is getting us nowhere. Let's go outside for a bit.'

They edged out of the caravan. The daylight seemed very bright after the gloomy interior. Dennis Saville had gone, but Sam Western's men were still there. They were throwing great heaps of vegetation out of the ditches. Matty seemed to have lost her fear of them and was grazing nearby.

'What are we going to do?' asked Mandy, sinking down on the caravan steps and breathing in the fresh air.

James sat down beside her. 'I don't know,' he admitted.

'If only we had time to tame the mother cat,'

Mandy said despairingly.

'Well, we haven't.' James looked at his watch. 'It's ten past twelve. We've got less than an hour.' He ran a hand through his hair. 'Look, I don't think we've got time to let the mother cat get used to us. We'll just have to get as close as we can and throw blankets over her so we can bundle her into the carrier. She won't like it, but it's better than being caught by Sam Western.'

Mandy didn't want to frighten the cat but James was right – they were fast running out of time. 'OK,' she said reluctantly. 'Let's get the blankets.'

When they came back to the field, the workmen were packing up for lunch. Matty was still standing near them but she was no longer grazing. Mandy frowned. There was something about the mare that seemed odd.

'James,' she said, stopping. 'Look at Matty.'

They both looked. Matty was standing absolutely still. Her neck was stretched out and all the muscles in her body looked stiff.

'She doesn't look well,' Mandy said in alarm.

They hurried towards Matty, slowing down when they were a few metres away so as not to frighten her, but she hardly seemed to notice them.

'Matty?' said Mandy.

The mare continued to stare straight ahead.

Mandy went up to her and put a hand on her neck. Matty didn't even look round. The muscles under her skin were twitching. Fear shot through Mandy. What was the matter with her? 'We'd better get Wilfred!' she gasped.

'I'll go,' James said. 'You stay here.'

As James tore off, Mandy moved to the mare's head. Matty's pupils looked wide and dilated. Something was very definitely wrong. Mandy looked round. Was it something Matty had eaten? But how could it be? Wilfred was always very careful to check the field for poisonous plants. She stroked the mare's face. 'It's OK, girl,' Mandy murmured, desperately wishing that James and Wilfred would hurry up.

'Is everything all right?' One of the workmen, passing nearby, suddenly seemed to notice that something was wrong.

Mandy shook her head. 'Matty's not well,' she said. 'But I don't know what's the matter.'

The workman came over, his kindly face creasing in concern. 'The old man owns her, doesn't he? Do you want me to fetch him?'

'My friend's just gone to get him,' Mandy said.

'What's up, Bill?' one of the other workmen asked, coming over.

'The horse is ill,' the man said.

Just then, to Mandy's relief, Wilfred and James appeared at the gate. 'Wilfred!' she shouted. 'Quick!'

Seeing Matty standing so stiffly, Wilfred started to run. By the time he reached her, he was wheezing loudly, his chest heaving with each breath. 'Matty, girl!' he gasped.

At the sound of her owner's voice, the mare turned her head slightly, one ear flickering. But it was obvious that even a little movement was an effort for her. Wilfred's eyes swept over her quivering skin, wide eyes and stiff legs. 'How long has she been like this?' he asked quickly.

'I don't know,' Mandy replied anxiously. 'We just noticed her when we were coming down the field. Do you know what the matter is?'

Wilfred's face was pale. 'Aye,' he replied, nodding. 'It's poisoning. No doubt about it.'

Five

Mandy, James and the workmen stared at Wilfred. 'But how can it be poisoning?' Mandy blurted out. 'You always check the field, Wilfred.'

'I know,' Wilfred said. 'I don't know what she's eaten but I know you don't get a horse looking like this unless it's been poisoned.'

Matty took one faltering step forwards and almost fell. James leaped beside Wilfred and together they managed to keep the mare on her feet by holding her headcollar firmly.

'Here, I'll help.' Bill, the first workman, moved forward quickly.

'Do you want me to call a vet?' his workmate offered. 'We've got a phone in the van.'

'Ring Animal Ark!' Mandy exclaimed. 'Tell them it's an emergency!' She reeled off the number, fear gripping her as she watched Matty stagger again. Whatever the poison was, it seemed to be acting very quickly.

The workman set off at a run up the field.

'Steady, girl!' Wilfred cried as Matty's legs shook. Mandy's heart contracted as she caught a glimpse of the mare's wide, frightened eyes. Matty seemed to be losing control of her muscles. *Hurry, please hurry!* she thought watching the workman sprint up the field.

She turned back to the ill mare. 'It's all right, Matty,' she said desperately. 'You're going to be OK.'

The grey mare staggered again and Mandy felt her heart skip a beat. What if Matty didn't last until her mum or dad got here? What if the poison was too strong?

'Mandy! It's your mum!' James gasped.

Mandy swung round. Emily Hope was walking through the campsite entrance. 'Mum!' Mandy cried in relief. She suddenly realised that her mum must have got the message about the cats and decided to call in. 'Mum! Quick! It's Matty! Wilfred thinks she's been poisoned!'

Mrs Hope broke into a run. In next to no time she had reached them. Her expert eyes swept over the mare's twitching muscles. 'You're right, Wilfred,' she said, moving forward to check Matty's gums and pupils. 'It looks like poisoning. Something's affecting her nerve cells and stimulating her central nervous system. Let me get my bag.' She ran back to the Land-rover.

Mandy stroked Matty with a trembling hand and forced herself to stay calm. Now her mum was here, surely everything would be all right.

'Right,' Mrs Hope said briskly as she came back and opened her bag. 'I'm going to give her a shot of anti-convulsives to help stop the spasms in her muscles but it's vital that we find out what the poison is.' She turned to Wilfred. 'Is there anything you can think of, Wilfred, that might have affected her like this?'

Wilfred shook his head. 'I check the whole field regularly.'

'When did her symptoms start?' Emily Hope

asked, taking a syringe and a phial of clear liquid out of her bag.

'It was Mandy and James who noticed her first,' Wilfred replied.

'She was fine earlier on,' Mandy said, remembering how Matty had been grazing happily when they had come out of the caravan. 'She was eating near the workmen. But then James and I went to get the blankets from the house and when we came back, we saw her looking ill.'

Emily Hope cleaned a square of hair on Matty's neck with a piece of cotton wool and inserted the needle. The grey mare didn't even seem to notice. Mrs Hope injected the anti-convulsive medicine and then turned to the workmen. 'Have you been using anything on the grass?' she asked. 'Any chemicals? Anything at all?'

Bill shook his head. 'We've just been clearing out the ditches, that's all.'

'The ditches?' Mrs Hope said quickly, glancing over to the piles of vegetation that the workmen had pulled up from the ditch round the side of the field. 'Did you dig out any water hemlock?' The workman looked confused. 'Cowbane is its other name. It's a tall, yellow-green plant with white flower heads made up of lots of little flowers.'

'Yeah, there was something like that,' Bill said. 'I thought it was just cow parsley. Tom, go and fetch some.' The other workman ran across to the pile of vegetation by the ditches.

'Cowbane?' Wilfred said, looking shocked. 'But that's deadly.'

Mrs Hope nodded. 'Its roots contain a toxic resin called cicutoxin that can be fatal to horses. It causes just the sort of symptoms Matty's got. It's my guess that when she was grazing near the ditches she picked up some of the roots that had been dug out.'

Just then, Tom returned with the plant. Its soil-covered roots showed white where the spades had cut through them. 'Isn't this just cow parsley?' he asked.

'No,' Mrs Hope said grimly. 'It's from the parsley family but it's cowbane – much more dangerous to horses.'

'Oh, Matty,' Wilfred groaned.

'Will she be OK, Mum?' Mandy asked, her heart pounding.

Her mum's worried green eyes met hers. 'I

don't know, love,' she said flatly. 'It depends how much she's eaten. If she's eaten a lot then the muscular spasms will lead to respiratory paralysis, which means that she won't be able to breathe.'

Mandy's heart clenched. 'There must be something you can do,' she said desperately.

'I can give her anti-convulsives to ease the spasms,' Mrs Hope said. 'But that's all. The next four to six hours will be crucial. If she survives those then there's every chance that she'll be OK.'

'But she might not survive them?' Mandy whispered, her mouth dry.

'No,' Mrs Hope said, taking a deep breath. 'I'm afraid she might not.'

The workmen stood around tensely, their lunch break forgotten. Emily Hope had told everyone to let Matty lie down and now the mare lay on the grass, her big grey body covered by a rug. Her head was stretched out and her muscles twitched spasmodically under her skin.

Mandy crouched beside Matty's neck, stroking her over and over again. Her mum had done all that she could and now it was just a question of waiting to see if the drugs would take effect.

Wilfred cradled Matty's head in his lap. 'I should have checked for cowbane in the ditches,' he muttered, his voice cracking. 'I could have kept her in her stable while the work was done.'

'You weren't to know,' Emily Hope said. 'It was just one of those things, Wilfred.'

'What would Rose say if she knew?' Wilfred whispered.

Mandy bit her lip as she saw the anguish in the old man's eyes. She knew that Matty had been his wife, Rose's, horse and it was partly because of this that the grey mare was so special to him. It was as though she still gave him a link with Rose. Mandy felt her own eyes sting with tears. *Please, Matty, get better,* she prayed desperately as she crouched beside Matty's neck.

Suddenly a loud voice cut through the air. 'What's all this then?'

Mandy looked up. Sam Western was striding towards them. Mandy realised with a jolt that it must be one o'clock. In the drama of the last hour, she had completely forgotten about the cat and her kittens.

'What's happened to the horse?' Sam Western demanded as he reached them. 'Is it ill?'

Mandy couldn't bear his tone. Before anyone could speak, she scrambled to her feet and faced Sam Western, her eyes blazing. 'Yes, she is!' she exclaimed. 'And it's all your fault!'

'My fault?' Sam Western echoed, looking taken aback. 'What on earth do you mean?'

'She ate some cowbane from the ditches,' Mandy told him, knowing that she was being irrational but simply not caring. 'You should have warned your men that it was poisonous to horses. You should have known!'

'That's enough, Mandy,' Emily Hope said, putting her hand on Mandy's arm. She turned to Sam Western. 'I'm afraid that Matty has eaten some water hemlock roots.'

Sam Western frowned. 'Will she get better?'

'As if you care!' Mandy shook away her mum's hand, the words bursting from her. 'You hate all animals!'

A pink flush spread over Sam Western's face. 'Now, that's not true. I don't hate animals,' he blustered.

'Yes you do!' Mandy cried. 'You always have! In fact,' she gasped as she looked at poor Matty's prone body beside her, 'you're probably *glad* that

Matty's ill!' With that, she turned and ran up the field.

Mandy didn't stop running until she reached the stable block. Throwing herself down on a bale of hay, she gave way to her tears. 'Oh, Matty!' she sobbed. 'Please don't die!'

There was the sound of footsteps behind her.

'Mandy?' It was her mum's voice.

For a moment, Mandy didn't move. She knew her mum would be furious with her for being so rude but she hadn't been able to stop herself. She continued to cry.

'Oh, Mandy,' her mum said in a quieter voice and Mandy felt her sit down beside her and put a hand on her shoulder.

She looked up, her face streaked with tears. 'I hate him, Mum,' she sobbed.

Mrs Hope pulled her close and stroked her hair. 'Matty being ill really isn't Sam Western's fault,' she said softly. 'He wasn't to know that there was cowbane in the ditches or that Matty would eat some before the men had a chance to clear it away.'

Mandy sniffed. 'He hates animals.'

'He doesn't hate them, love. He just sees

animals very differently from the way we do.' Mrs Hope sighed. 'But that certainly doesn't give you the right to speak to him like you did.' Mandy glanced up at her. 'You're going to have to apologise.'

'No!' Mandy exclaimed, pulling back from her mum and staring at her in horror. 'No! I won't!'

'Yes, you will,' Emily Hope said firmly.

'It's not fair!' she protested, but she knew deep down that her mum was right.

Her mum simply stood up and motioned towards the door.

Mandy walked reluctantly down the field. She saw James look at her anxiously but she didn't say anything to him. Red in the face but holding her head high, she marched up to Sam Western. 'I'm sorry,' she muttered, trying to sound as if she meant it.

To Mandy's surprise, Sam Western looked almost embarrassed. 'That's all right,' he said awkwardly. He cleared his throat and looked at Mrs Hope who had crouched beside Matty again to check her breathing and heart rate. 'How's the mare doing, Mrs Hope?'

'Well, she's not getting any worse,' Emily Hope said, looking slightly relieved. 'We're just going to have to see what happens over the next few hours.'

Sam Western turned to the men. 'Clear the site and then take the rest of the afternoon off. I don't want you disturbing the horse. It will be better if we get out of your way,' he said quickly to Emily Hope and Wilfred. 'But if there's anything you need,' he cleared his throat again, 'just let me know.'

Mandy stared in surprise as Sam Western turned and strode towards his car. He had almost sounded as though he cared what happened to

Matty. For a moment, she was too stunned to move but then she remembered something. 'Mr Western!' she called, jumping to her feet. 'What about the cats?'

Sam Western stopped. For a moment he seemed to hesitate. 'They can stay until Sunday,' he said quickly. 'We'll leave sorting out that caravan to last.' A more familiar frown crossed his face. 'But if they're not out then . . .'

'They will be!' Mandy gasped, looking at James in astonishment. Sunday was almost a whole week away. She was sure they could tempt the mother cat out by then. 'Thank you!'

Without another word, Sam Western strode to his car.

Mandy kneeled down beside James. 'Did you hear that? He's given us until Sunday!'

'Guilty conscience,' James muttered darkly.

Mandy stroked Matty's neck. The mare's breathing seemed slightly easier but her muscles still twitched. 'Is there anything else we can do, Mum?' she asked anxiously.

Emily Hope shook her head. 'Not at the moment.' She took her phone from her pocket. 'I'll ring the surgery and let Jean know where I am,' she said. She walked away a few paces and punched in the number.

Mandy looked at Wilfred. The old man's face was furrowed as he stared down at Matty. Mandy moved closer to him and squeezed his gnarled hand. 'She'll be all right, Wilfred,' she said. 'She'll get better.'

Wilfred continued to watch the grey mare closely. 'Thanks, lass,' he said, at last. He placed his hand gently on Matty's velvety nose. 'I don't know what I'd do without my girl.' He shook his head. 'I remember the day she was born. A skinny little thing with great long legs. It was Rose who delivered her.' He smiled at the memory. 'She was always more Rose's horse than mine. It was Rose who broke her in and Rose who started her off in the riding-school.' A shadow crossed Wilfred's face. 'Now Rose is gone and Matty's all that I have left. I know that she's getting on in years and that one day she'll die but not yet, surely . . .' His words trailed off as he looked at the grey mare.

Mandy didn't know what to say and, looking at James, she could tell that he felt the same. The worry on Wilfred's face was awful to see. She stroked Matty's neck, wishing that there was something more she could do.

The minutes slowly ticked by into hours. Matty didn't get any better but at the same time she didn't seem to be getting any worse. After a while, Mandy's mum went to Wilfred's cottage and made some lunch and coffee for them all. But the tray remained barely touched. No one felt like eating much when Matty was so ill.

Suddenly, James jumped to his feet. 'I'll go and put some water in the caravan for the cats,' he said. 'Now we've blocked the escape route, the mother cat will need us to provide her with food and water. Are you coming?' he said to Mandy.

Mandy shook her head. Although she understood James's urge to do something rather than just sit round waiting, she couldn't bring herself to leave Matty's side. She watched James hurry away.

'We should check Matty's pulse again,' Emily Hope said.

'I'll do it,' Mandy said quickly. She took the stethoscope from her mum and placed it just behind Matty's elbow, as she'd been shown before.

Looking at her watch, she counted how many heartbeats she could hear in a minute. 'Fifty,' she said to her mum, as she took the stethoscope from her ears.

'That's good,' her mum said. 'It's almost within the normal range.'

Mandy leaned forward and lifted Matty's lips. She remembered her mum saying that pale gums, like a rapid or weakened pulse, were an indicator of shock. 'Her gums are better, too,' she said, showing Matty's pink gums to her mum. 'And I'm sure the spasms are getting less.'

Emily Hope patted Matty's damp neck. 'Come on, girl. You can do it. You've just got to keep fighting.'

James returned a few minutes later. 'The cats are OK,' he told them. 'The mother's eaten all the cat food that was in the bowl and she seems a bit calmer. I gave her some water but we should remember to leave some more food for her tonight.'

'So you've got until Sunday to get them out?' Mrs Hope said.

Mandy nodded. 'Do you think we'll be able to?'

'I think you've got a good chance,' her mum

replied. 'Just take it slowly. Spend as much time with them as you can. With the mother being shut in, she will rely on you for food. Feed her several times a day and hopefully she should start to accept you and look forward to your visits. But don't let her out of the caravan. If you do she may move the kittens again, or even take fright and abandon them.'

'I still can't believe that Sam Western's given us more time,' James said.

Mandy shivered. 'I wonder what he'd have done with the cats if he'd taken them away today.'

'Killed them probably,' James said grimly. 'You saw his face when he heard that the cats were trapped in the caravan. I bet he just thinks they're pests that need to be dealt with.'

'Look!' Wilfred said suddenly.

Mandy, James and Mrs Hope looked round. Matty had raised her head from the grass. With a struggle, she heaved herself from her side on to her stomach. The cats were instantly forgotten. 'Matty!' Mandy gasped.

The grey mare looked round. Her muscles gave the occasional tremble but Mandy could see that her eyes had lost their wide, staring look.

A relieved smile lit up Emily Hope's face. 'She's fought off the poison! She's going to pull through.'

Mandy could hardly believe it. A wave of delight overwhelmed her and she flung her arms round James. For once he didn't look embarrassed. 'Matty's going to be OK!' he gasped, his glasses falling down his nose.

Mandy didn't think she had ever felt happier. 'Wilfred!' she cried, swinging round. 'Matty's going to make it!'

Wilfred was still kneeling by the mare. He placed a shaky hand on Matty's head. 'Oh, Matty,' he said, his voice cracking with emotion. 'I don't know how I'd have coped if you hadn't pulled through.'

Lifting her nostrils to Wilfred's hair, Matty blew gently, affection for her owner shining in her dark eyes.

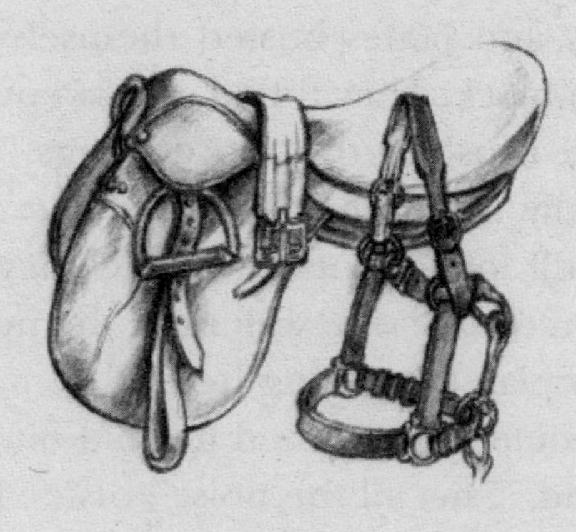

Six

As soon as Emily Hope was sure that Matty was on the mend, she set off for Animal Ark. 'Ring me if she shows any signs of a relapse,' she told Wilfred, as he led Matty into her stable. 'Otherwise I'll come and check on her after this afternoon's surgery.' She smiled at Mandy and James. 'I'll collect you then. Take good care of Matty.'

'As if we'd do anything else,' Mandy said, putting her arms round Matty's neck and giving her a hug.

Wilfred wanted to stay in the stable with Matty,

so Mandy and James busied themselves round the stable block. They tidied and swept the feed store and brushed the mare's rugs, stopping occasionally to go and check on the cats. The mother still looked unsettled and they decided that it would be best to wait until the next day to start their plan for taming her.

'She should have calmed down a bit by then,' Mandy said. 'I bet all the noise outside has upset her even more.'

At the end of the day, Wilfred came out of Matty's stable. 'You've done a grand job,' he said, looking round at the folded rugs, clean tack and freshly swept floor. 'Thank you.'

'That's all right,' Mandy said, smiling. 'We're just glad to help.'

James glanced at his watch. 'We should feed the cats,' he said. 'Your mum will be back soon.'

They filled a plastic scoop with the cat food which they had brought from Animal Ark and made their way to the caravan. The cat was lying down, feeding her kittens, but as soon as they walked in, she sprang to her feet and hissed warningly at them. The kittens mewed in protest at having their meal interrupted. Shuffling after her, they butted their heads underneath her belly, searching for her teats. The mother stayed absolutely still, her eyes riveted on Mandy and James.

Trying not to make any sudden movements in case he frightened her, James edged forward and poured the contents of the scoop into the empty bowl. 'We'll have to try and clean this place up a bit tomorrow,' he said, wrinkling his nose at the heavy smell of cats in the air.

Mandy nodded. 'We can bring some newspaper and cover the floor,' she said. 'Then we can clean it out each day.' She checked the cat's water. It was still full. As she looked up, she met the cat's suspicious amber gaze. 'You'll be all right here,' Mandy said softly, wishing that the cat didn't look as if she disliked them so much. 'We're your friends. We'll take care of you and your kittens.' The cat drew back slightly, her ears flattening against the sides of her head. She looked like the last thing she wanted was for Mandy and James to be her friends.

A sudden shiver of foreboding ran down Mandy's spine. Standing there, so warily, the cat looked completely wild. Were they really going to be able to tame her in so short a time?

Getting out of the Land-rover at Animal Ark that evening, after they'd dropped James off, Mandy felt her legs wobble with exhaustion. It had been a very long, action-packed day. So much had happened – the cats disappearing, Sam Western's threats, Matty being ill. Mandy rubbed a hand across her eyes. It seemed like a lifetime since they had set off that morning with such high hopes of catching the cats.

'Supper, then an early bed for you, Mandy Hope,' her mum said, looking at her in concern.

Mandy nodded, too tired to argue. But as she reached the back door, she remembered something. 'Dylan!' she exclaimed. 'How is he?'

Her mum smiled. 'There's been a slight improvement today,' she replied. 'He lifted his head for the first time.'

Mandy immediately forgot her tiredness. 'Can I see him?' she asked excitedly.

'Come on, then,' her mum said. 'Just for a few minutes.'

They went to the residential unit. As Emily

Hope unlocked the door, Mandy heard a faint whimper. She glanced at her mum.

'Yes, that's him,' Mrs Hope said.

Mandy hurried through the door. Dylan was still lying down but when he saw her, his ears pricked up and he slowly lifted his head. Mandy reached into the puppy's cage and he stretched his muzzle towards her. 'You *are* looking better,' Mandy said, greatly relieved to see him looking so much more alert.

'Now we just have to get him on to his feet,' Mrs Hope said, leaning over Mandy's shoulder. 'He still doesn't seem to want to stand. And I wish he looked happier, the poor little mite.'

As Mandy rubbed Dylan under his ears, she remembered what she had thought the night before. 'Maybe he's missing his owners.'

Her mum nodded. 'Maybe. We hadn't wanted them to visit until he showed some signs of recovery in case it over-stimulated him. But now he's looking a bit brighter, it might do him good to see them. I'll give them a ring this evening and see if they can pop in tomorrow.'

'Dad, have you got any more ideas about how

James and I could tame the cat?' Mandy asked as she helped her dad clear up after supper. 'We haven't had much luck with her, so far.'

Adam Hope considered the question as he began to rinse the pans. 'Well, obviously feeding her is important, and you should keep your body language as unthreatening as possible. That means no sudden movements, and make sure you speak in a low voice,' he explained. 'And don't look her directly in the eye or face her straight on. To a cat or dog, that's like giving a direct challenge. So keep your eyes lowered and turn your shoulders at an angle to her.'

Mandy nodded. All her dad's advice made sense. She put away the pans and began to make a mental list of the things she and James would need the next day – dried cat food, a clean food bowl, newspapers for the floor.

Just then, her mum came back in from ringing Dylan's owners, Sam and Liz Butler. 'The Butlers are coming to see Dylan tomorrow afternoon,' she announced. 'I spoke to Liz. She sounded as though she could hardly wait.'

'Oh, good,' Mandy said, pleased.

Her mum smiled. 'Why don't you go to bed, love? You look shattered.'

Mandy nodded. Her eyelids felt very heavy. ''Night,' she said, going across to her mum and dad and kissing them.

''Night, love,' her dad replied. 'Sweet dreams.'

When Mandy woke up the next morning, it seemed unusually light outside. She glanced at her bedside clock and saw that it was quarter past eight! She had overslept by an hour and a half.

She jumped out of bed and threw on some clothes, then ran downstairs. Her mum was just about to go into the surgery. 'I'm sorry!' Mandy gasped. Normally she was up in time to clean out the cages in the residential unit and help give the patients their medication.

'It's OK,' Emily Hope said. 'I thought it best to let you sleep in. Simon and I have seen to the animals.' She smiled. 'And there's good news from Wilfred. He rang ten minutes ago to say that Matty's had a good night and is looking much brighter.'

Mandy felt a weight lift from her shoulders. 'That's brilliant!'

Emily Hope expertly twisted her long red hair into a knot at the nape of neck, securing it with a slide. 'Now, why don't you have some breakfast and then come and give Simon a hand?' she suggested as she headed for the door.

Mandy quickly ate a piece of toast and honey, then ran through to the surgery. Simon had just finished mopping the floor. 'That was good timing,' he grinned, squeezing the mop out in the bucket

'Sorry, I overslept,' Mandy apologised.

'I'll forgive you,' Simon said. 'But only if you empty this bucket for me.'

Mandy took the bucket of dirty water from him. 'Slave driver!' she teased.

She was emptying the bucket outside when she saw a dark-haired man help Mrs Austin get out of a blue van in the car park. The man then lifted out Mrs Austin's spaniel, Archie, and put him down gently on to the ground.

Mandy went over. 'Hello, Mrs Austin,' she said, 'Has Archie come in for his X-rays?' She stroked the dog's soft, floppy ears.

The elderly lady nodded. 'I hope we're not too early.'

'No, you're right on time,' Mandy said. 'Come in.'

She fetched Simon, who gave Mrs Austin a form to fill in, and then they took Archie through to the residential unit.

Mandy was pleased to see Dylan look up as they entered. She fetched a piece of sheepskin and put it in the cage next to the puppy. 'There we are, Archie,' she said, carefully lifting the dog into the cage and unclipping his lead.

Mrs Austin reached out and stroked her dog's

head with a trembling hand. 'Be a good boy,' she whispered to him.

'We'll look after him,' Simon said kindly. 'Don't worry, Mrs Austin. He's in safe hands.'

The old lady nodded and then, with one last look at Archie, she left.

Seven

It had been a busy morning at Animal Ark, but it was just starting to quieten down when James arrived. 'Are you ready?' he asked Mandy.

'Yep,' she replied. She poked her head into her mum's consultation room. 'Is it OK if I go to Wilfred's now?'

Her mum looked up from the insurance form she was filling in for a patient. 'Fine. Tell him I'll call in later to check on Matty.'

Mandy nodded and then she and James loaded their bikes with cat food, newspapers and cleaning equipment, and set off for Wilfred's.

The February sun was shining down and white clouds blew briskly across a forget-me-not blue sky. Mandy felt her spirits lift. On a day like this, she couldn't help but feel optimistic. Surely the cat would soon see that she and James meant her family no harm?

Wilfred was in Matty's stable when they arrived. 'How's Matty?' Mandy asked quickly.

'See for yourself,' Wilfred said, opening the door for her.

Matty was pulling at a haynet but, hearing the door open, she looked round, her ears pricked and her eyes bright.

'She looks loads better!' James said.

Mandy dumped the armload of cat things that she was carrying, then went and patted the mare. 'Hello, girl,' she said. Matty snuffled her hair affectionately.

'She's thanking you for helping her yesterday,' Wilfred said.

Mandy laughed, but in a way, it almost felt as if Wilfred was right.

'So, we'll feed the mother first,' James said, as they left the stable block and headed for the caravan, discussing their plans for taming the cat. 'Then we'll wait a bit for her to settle down before we clean out the mess and put some newspaper down.'

'Keeping the door shut so she can't escape,' Mandy added, 'and keeping our bodies turned sideways on to her so she doesn't feel threatened.' She put her hand on the door of the caravan. 'Are you ready?'

James nodded. Mandy opened the door and they slipped inside.

The kittens had obviously been playing in the middle of the floor but, at the sound of the door opening, they scampered over to their mother at the back of the caravan. Hiding behind her, they peeked out at Mandy and James with their big blue eyes. The mother cat arched her back warningly.

Being careful not to look directly at her, Mandy and James refilled the food bowl and the saucer of water and pushed them towards her. Then they sat down and waited to see what would happen.

At first, the mother cat stayed where she was, but they could tell by the way her whiskers twitched and her eyes flickered every now and then to the bowl that she was interested in the food. Finally, her hunger seemed to get the better of her. Keeping a wary eye on Mandy and James, she ran to the food and, crouching down beside it, began to eat.

The kittens came to investigate the food bowl. As always, the black one was first. 'They're too young to eat solid food yet, aren't they?' James said in a low voice, as the kittens dipped their heads into the bowl, sniffed the food and then stumbled away on their short, unsteady legs.

Mandy nodded. 'Yes. Kittens normally start eating proper food when they're about five weeks old.'

Uninterested in the food, the kittens started to play. They were still unco-ordinated, and as they tried to bat each other with their front paws they over-balanced and rolled on to the floor.

'The black one's the liveliest,' Mandy said, watching the black kitten tussle with the male grey-and-white kitten and then spring away and bounce at the smaller female kitten who was sitting watching them play.

James grinned at the kittens' antics. 'We should think of names for them,' he said.

'You're right,' Mandy agreed. 'Any ideas?'

James studied the kittens. 'Well, the two grey-and-white ones look like they've been climbing up a chimney,' he said. 'How about calling the female, Smudge, and the male, Sweep?'

Mandy nodded enthusiastically. She liked the names. 'Yes, and the black one could be . . .'

'Sooty!' they both said at precisely the same time.

Mandy grinned. 'That's settled then.'

'Not yet,' James said. 'There's still the mother. We need something to go with Sooty, Smudge and Sweep.' He frowned for a moment. 'Smoke?' he suggested, admiring the mother's beautiful grey coat.

'Too like Smokey,' Mandy said, thinking of her gran and grandad's young cat. 'How about Ash?'

James shook his head. 'Too boyish. What about Cinders?'

Mandy loved it. 'Brilliant!' she exclaimed. 'Cinders, Sooty, Smudge and Sweep. You're a genius, James!'

'I know,' James grinned. 'It's hard, but I just can't help it.'

Mandy hit him playfully. 'Idiot!'

The sudden movement made Cinders look up quickly from her saucer of water. Mandy immediately froze. To her relief, Cinders didn't run off. She stared at them for a moment with enormous amber eyes and then lowered her head and licked up the last few drops.

'She doesn't seem quite so scared of us,' Mandy whispered to James.

'I know,' he said, as Cinders trotted back to her nest at the back of the caravan.

They waited until Cinders settled down and then began to clean the floor. Cinders watched them warily, but she didn't leave the nest. Soon the floor was clean and covered with a layer of newspaper. Mandy didn't want to disturb Cinders by going too near the nest and so she pushed a piece of paper across the floor until it was almost touching the kittens.

Cinders backed off with a suspicious hiss but Sooty spotted the corner of the moving sheet of paper and sprang on it playfully. Sweep joined him. Together they tussled with the corner, their tiny claws scratching through the paper.

'Look at Smudge, watching,' Mandy whispered.

Smudge was sitting in the nest, her eyes wide in

alarm, but her head moved from side to side as she followed her brothers' movements. She was the quietest of the three kittens. She looked as if she wanted to join in but didn't quite dare to. Finally, however, she couldn't resist. With a high-pitched mew, she sprang at Sooty's waving tail.

'They're so adorable,' Mandy said, as the three kittens tumbled over each other, scrunching up the clean paper. 'They deserve really good homes after such a bad start in life.'

An hour later, Mandy and James left the caravan and went to Matty's stable. Mrs Hope had arrived and was talking to Wilfred. 'How are the cats this morning?' she asked as they came in.

'OK,' Mandy said. 'Though the mum's still really nervous of us. What about Matty?'

'She seems to be making a perfect recovery,' Emily Hope said. 'I was just telling Wilfred that she'll need to take it easy for a few days – so no riding this half-term, I'm afraid – but she can go out in the field as long as there are absolutely no more cowbane roots lying about.'

'We'll check for you, Wilfred,' James offered quickly. 'Come on, Mandy.'

Before Mandy followed, she remembered something that had been at the back of her mind all morning. 'Mum, how's Archie?' she asked. 'Have you found out what's wrong with him?'

'Dad was just X-raying him as I came out,' her mum replied. Her eyes met Mandy's. 'Remember, Archie's old, love. It may not be good news.'

'I hope he *is* OK,' Mandy said, thinking of Mrs Austin's worried face.

'So do I,' her mum said.

After waving Mrs Hope off, Mandy and James went down the field and began to scour the grass near the ditches for uprooted cowbane, but the workmen seemed to have cleared up well.

'I still can't believe that Sam Western didn't warn the workmen about cowbane,' Mandy said angrily. 'He knew Matty was in the field.'

'He might not have known that it was poisonous to horses,' James said, trying to be fair. 'And he did offer to help when he found out that Matty was ill.'

'He probably just didn't want to look bad in front of his men,' Mandy said. 'You know, he doesn't care about animals one bit.' She shivered.

'Just imagine what he'd do if he got his hands on Cinders and her kittens.'

James nodded. 'Yeah, I know.' He frowned. 'I hope they end up with people who will love them and look after them properly.'

Mandy agreed. 'I wish I could have one,' she said longingly. But it was impossible. Life at Animal Ark was just too busy.

'Me too,' James said. 'But Mum and Dad would never agree. They think that Blackie and Eric are enough.' Eric, James's young cat, had himself been part of another litter of kittens that they had rescued.

'Oh well,' Mandy went on, determined not to look on the downside. 'It's too soon to be thinking about permanent homes for them. We have to get them out of the caravan first.'

Mandy and James spent most of the day in the caravan. But even though Cinders appeared to be slightly more relaxed with them, she still seemed determined not to let them anywhere near her. Whenever they tried to approach her, she arched her back and spat warningly.

'Maybe she'll be better tomorrow,' James said

hopefully, as they walked up the field that afternoon.

Mandy sighed. 'Maybe.'

'We could buy some treats and try tempting her with them,' James suggested.

Mandy liked the idea. 'OK,' she said. 'Let's buy some at the post office tomorrow.'

After saying goodbye to Wilfred, they cycled back into the village.

'I'd better go and walk Blackie,' James said, stopping his bike at the village green. 'He can't understand why he's not allowed to come with me each day, but I don't want to risk him frightening the cats.'

'See you tomorrow,' Mandy said. Then she carried on to Animal Ark.

As she swung into the drive, her feet suddenly slowed on the pedals and she skidded to a stop. Her mum was helping Mrs Austin into the same blue van that Mandy had seen that morning. Mrs Austin was clutching a collar and lead and looked as if she was crying.

Mandy suddenly felt sick. Where was Archie? Dropping her bike on the ground, she ran over to her mum, who was watching the van pull away.

'Mum!' Mandy gasped. 'What's happened to Archie?'

Mrs Hope looked at her sadly and took her hand. 'He's been put down, love.'

'Why?' Mandy gasped.

'The X-rays showed that he had an advanced bone tumour,' her mum explained quietly. 'It was inoperable and he was in pain. When Mrs Austin came in, she decided that the kindest thing was to put Archie to sleep before he suffered any more.'

For a moment, Mandy couldn't speak. She knew that it was impossible to cure every animal who came into Animal Ark, but it didn't make it any easier when an animal was put down.

Her mum seemed to understand how she was feeling. 'It was for the best, love. He'd had a long and happy life and it wouldn't have been fair to let him suffer.'

Mandy knew she was right but it still seemed so unfair. 'Will . . . will Mrs Austin get another dog?' she asked.

'I don't think so,' her mum said. 'I asked her that and she said that she didn't think she could bear to have one after having Archie for so long.'

Just then, Jean Knox put her head out of the door. 'There's a phone call for you, Emily.'

'OK, I'm coming,' Mrs Hope called back. She looked at Mandy. 'It's been quite hectic this afternoon. Can you come and help?' she asked.

Mandy guessed that her mum wanted to keep her busy so that she wouldn't think about Archie too much. 'OK,' she said.

She put her bike away and went into the surgery. As usual, there was lots to do, and as she threw herself into the work she found that the familiar tasks did provide some sort of comfort.

Just as the surgery was finishing, Sam and Liz Butler, Dylan's owners, arrived. They looked pale and anxious.

'We've come to see Dylan,' Liz said to Jean Knox. 'Mrs Hope rang us last night.'

'I'll just get her,' Jean said.

As Jean went to fetch Emily Hope, Mandy entered the residential unit to check on Dylan. The puppy was lying sadly on his blanket. She opened the door of the cage and stroked his soft head. 'You've got visitors, boy,' she said. 'Cheer up.'

But Dylan just stared at her with mournful brown eyes.

Emily Hope led Mr and Mrs Butler through to the residential unit.

'How is he?' Mandy heard Sam Butler say.

In his cage, Dylan started and pricked his ears. Mandy stood back so that he could see his owners.

'He's improving slightly,' Emily Hope said, opening the door to the unit. 'But he's still very quiet.'

'Dylan?' Liz Butler said, coming in cautiously. Mandy saw her eyes widen as she took in the stitches and swollen skin along her puppy's shaved neck. 'Oh, Dylan!' She rushed up to the cage.

For a moment, Dylan stared as if he couldn't believe what he was seeing. Then with a high-pitched whimper of delight, he stretched out his front paws.

'Mum! Look!' Mandy gasped, as the puppy scrambled unsteadily to his feet.

Sam Butler came and stood beside his wife. 'Hello, boy,' he said.

With another whimper, Dylan stumbled towards them. His back legs almost seemed to give way, but with an enormous effort he managed to stay

on his feet. Reaching Liz and Sam, he began to lick them ecstatically.

Tears of happiness sprang to Mandy's eyes.

'I think you were right, Mandy,' her mum said softly, coming over and putting an arm round her shoulders. 'This was just the medicine Dylan needed.'

Looking at the joy on the Butlers' faces and at Dylan's frantically wagging tail, Mandy knew that there was nothing she wanted more in the world than to be a vet, like her mum and dad.

Eight

The next morning, Mandy told James all about Dylan as they cycled to the post office to buy some treats for Cinders.

'He's going home this afternoon,' she told him. 'Liz and Sam, his owners, are going to take some time off work to look after him.'

'That's brilliant!' James said, stopping his bike outside the post office.

Mandy nodded. 'I know. I'll miss him, but I'm just really glad he's going to get better.'

The bell on the post office's door tinkled as they walked in. As well as being a post office it was a general store that seemed to sell just about everything anyone could want to buy. Mrs McFarlane, the postmistress, was tidying the shelves. 'Hello, you two,' she said with her usual ready smile. 'What can I get you today?'

'Some cat treats, please, Mrs McFarlane,' James replied.

Mrs McFarlane wiped her hands on her gaily striped apron and climbed up her stepladder. 'Are they for Eric?' she asked, taking down a box of treats.

James shook his head. 'They're for a stray cat we've found. We're trying to tame her,' he said.

'The cat and her three kittens are living in one of the caravans on Sam Western's campsite,' Mandy explained. 'Sam Western won't let them stay there, so we want to take them somewhere safe. But we have to win the mother cat's trust, first.'

Mrs McFarlane shook her head. 'I sometimes wonder what the animals round Welford would do without the pair of you.' She handed the treats to James. 'Go on, you can have them for nothing,' she said, seeing him dig in his pocket for some money. 'It's in a good cause.'

'Oh, thanks, Mrs McFarlane!' James exclaimed.

Just then, the post office door opened and Ernie Bell came in. Ernie had lived in the village all his life and he was good friends with Mandy's grandfather. He nodded at Mandy and James. 'Morning,' he said shortly.

'Hi, Ernie,' Mandy said cheerfully. She knew better than to be put off by Ernie's gruff exterior. He had often helped her and James in the past – building fences, releasing rabbits into the wild and even adopting a squirrel.

'Mandy and James were just telling me about a stray cat they've been trying to catch,' Mrs McFarlane said, keen as usual to pass on village news. 'Up at Sam Western's campsite. In one of his caravans.'

Ernie raised his eyebrows. 'In one of the caravans? I bet young Sam Western hasn't taken too kindly to that,' he said.

'No, he hasn't. That's why we're trying to move her,' Mandy explained.

She and James stepped away from the counter as Ernie bought his morning paper, and then followed him outside into the warm sunshine.

'Mrs McFarlane's just given us these,' James

said, holding out the foil-wrapped treats for Ernie to see. 'We thought we could tempt her near us.'

Ernie peered at them. 'Salmon-flavoured,' he read from the packet. He sniffed scornfully. 'You don't need new-fangled things like that. All you need is a bit of catnip.'

'Catnip?' Mandy echoed. She knew that catnip was a green herb that lots of cats loved to sniff and play in.

'Aye, catnip,' Ernie said. 'You mark my words, take some into this caravan with you and that cat will soon be rolling over and playing like a kitten.'

'Well, we could try it as well. Where can we get some?' Mandy asked.

'Try your grandad, lass. He's bound to have some in that garden of his.'

Mandy was sure that Ernie was right. Her grandad was a very keen gardener and grew all sorts of herbs, vegetables and flowers in his garden. 'OK, we will,' she said, looking at James, who nodded.

They said goodbye to Ernie and cycled round to Lilac Cottage, where Mandy's grandparents lived. Snowdrops nodded in terracotta pots round the door. Mandy rapped on the knocker.

A few moments later, her gran opened the door. She was wearing a bright turquoise tracksuit. 'Mandy! James!' she said, her face splitting into a broad smile. 'What a nice surprise. You should have told me you were coming, I was just off to the village hall to play badminton with Margaret Davy.'

'It's OK, Gran,' Mandy said, kissing her. 'We're not going to stay for long. Is Grandad here?'

Gran looked over her shoulder. 'Tom!' she called. 'Mandy and James want to see you. Come in to the kitchen,' she said to them. 'He'll be through in a minute.'

They followed her into the cosy kitchen. 'Now sit down,' said Gran, opening her biscuit tin. 'And have a biscuit. Ginger ones – baked yesterday.'

Mandy and James helped themselves from the tin. 'Thanks, Gran,' Mandy said. 'These look delicious.'

Her gran looked pleased. 'So, what do you want with your grandad?' she asked, sitting down opposite them.

Before Mandy could reply, her grandad came through to the kitchen. He smiled when he saw them. 'Good morning, you two,' he said cheerfully. 'What can I do for you?'

Mandy and James quickly explained about Cinders and her kittens and about meeting Ernie in the post office. 'He said we should try taking some catnip into the caravan,' Mandy said, through a mouthful of biscuit. 'And so we were wondering if you had any.'

Grandad Hope nodded. 'I've got several clumps of it,' he said. 'The bees love it in the summer. If you come into the garden, I'll cut you some.'

'Great!' said Mandy, hastily finishing her biscuit. 'Come on, James!'

'I'll see you soon,' Gran called from the doorway as Mandy and James followed Grandad into the garden. 'I've got to dash or Margaret will think I've forgotten her.'

'Bye!' Mandy waved as her gran set off with her sports bag in one hand and her badminton racket in the other. Sometimes, Mandy wondered if her gran had ever heard the term 'a quiet retirement'. If she wasn't playing badminton, or sitting on committees, she was baking cakes for the Women's Institute or setting out on yet another holiday with Grandad in their smart camper van.

'Here we are,' Grandad said, stopping by a low

green bush. 'Catnip, otherwise known as *Nepeta cataria.*'

'It looks like mint,' James said, looking at the small, veined leaves.

'That's because it is a member of the mint family,' Grandad Hope agreed. He picked off a couple of leaves and handed them to Mandy and James to smell. 'Now, if you wait here, I'll get some secateurs.'

Mandy and James soon had a plastic carrier bag full of catnip cuttings. 'Thanks, Grandad,' Mandy said, as they picked up their bikes.

'Any time,' Grandad Hope smiled. 'I just hope it does the trick. Not all cats love catnip, you know. Some of them go wild for it, but others don't seem to have the slightest interest. I asked your dad about it once and he said that some cats are simply born unable to detect the smell.'

'I hope Cinders can smell it,' James said to Mandy.

'Me too,' she agreed.

'Cinders will be ready for her breakfast,' Mandy said, when she and James finally reached the campsite. 'It's quite late.'

They fetched a scoop of dried food and some fresh newspapers from the supplies they had left in the feed room and walked over to the caravan, which looked cosy and cheerful in the bright morning sun.

The cats were in their nest. Cinders stood up as they entered. But, this time, she didn't shrink back. She stood her ground, her amber eyes flickering to the scoop that James was carrying. He started to pour the food into the empty bowl.

'Look!' Mandy whispered. James glanced up. Cinders was creeping towards him, her eyes fixed on the dry food. She stopped warily a couple of metres away.

Very quietly, James stepped back a pace. It was enough to give Cinders confidence. Bounding forward, she began to gobble down the food in great hungry mouthfuls.

'She's definitely getting tamer,' James whispered.

Mandy nodded, hope brimming up inside her. Maybe this would be the day that they got Cinders and her family out of the caravan.

While Cinders ate, Sooty and Sweep came over to investigate Mandy and James. Sweep pounced on Mandy's hand, clawing at it and overbalancing. She laughed and tickled his fluffy white tummy. 'Come on, Smudge,' she said, seeing the other grey-and-white kitten sitting a little way off, watching. 'Come and play.' Mandy wriggled her fingers invitingly on the floor.

Smudge hesitated for a moment and then plucked up her courage and trotted over.

'They're so cute!' James said, picking Sooty up and letting the lively black kitten claw all the way up his jumper to his shoulder.

It didn't take long for Cinders to finish her food. She went back to the nest, stretched, and then lay down. The kittens immediately bounded over and, snuggling underneath her, they began to feed.

Moving quietly so as not to disturb them, Mandy and James removed the dirty papers and replaced them with clean sheets. 'That's better,' Mandy said at last, looking round the caravan with a feeling of satisfaction. She nudged James. 'Look.' Full of milk, the kittens had curled up together and gone to sleep.

'We could bring the treats and the catnip in,' James suggested, 'and see if we can get Cinders to come close to us while the kittens are sleeping.

She's looking quite relaxed.'

Mandy nodded and fetched the bag from outside. As she opened it, the minty smell of the freshly-cut catnip filled the caravan.

'Mmm, it smells delicious,' James said, sniffing.

'Let's hope Cinders thinks so too,' Mandy said, glancing at the grey cat.

'She *looks* interested,' James said. Cinders had sat up and was staring at them. 'Let's put some on the floor and see what she does.'

Taking the catnip out of the bag, they spread it out on the floor. Then they sat down nearby to watch.

Cinders's whiskers twitched as she breathed in the sweet scent of the herb. Suddenly, she opened her mouth and curled back her upper lip.

'Eric does that sometimes,' James whispered, remembering his own cat reacting in the same way.

'Yes, I've seen him,' Mandy whispered back. 'Dad told me that cats do it when they smell something interesting. They trap the smell on their tongue and then press their tongue against the roof of their mouth. It's like a cross between tasting and smelling.'

'She's coming over,' James said.

They both held their breath as Cinders edged across the floor towards the catnip. She stopped every few seconds to glance at Mandy and James, but as neither of them moved she seemed to gain in courage. Reaching the catnip, she lowered her head and sniffed delicately at the minty leaves. It was the closest she had ever been to them, but she seemed too intrigued by the catnip to care.

Mandy watched, entranced, as Cinders chewed one of the leaves and then crouched down and rubbed her head against the stalks. Suddenly, the little cat threw herself down on the ground and rolled over and over. Jumping to her feet, she miaowed excitedly.

It was the first time Mandy had seen Cinders look so playful and relaxed. With her amber eyes alight, she looked almost like a kitten again. Mandy was even more determined that Cinders should have a good home – a home where she would be loved and cared for to make up for the hard start she'd had in life.

'Do you think we can get closer to her?' James whispered eagerly.

Mandy looked at Cinders, who was sniffing the

leaves again. 'I'll try,' she replied.

She waited until Cinders looked relaxed and then she leaned forward. The grey cat was so close that she could almost touch her. Holding her breath, Mandy reached out. For one moment, her fingers hovered over Cinders's back but suddenly the little cat noticed how near she was. Cinders froze and then, leaping into the air, she fled to the back of the caravan.

'Oh!' Mandy exclaimed in frustration.

'You were so close,' James groaned.

Mandy pushed a hand through her hair. 'Now what do we do?' She looked at Cinders who was crouching in the corner, staring at them with fear in her eyes.

'Try some treats?' James suggested.

Keen to try anything that might get them close to Cinders again, Mandy opened the packet of salmon-flavoured treats and scattered a few round the food bowl and over the floor in front of them.

'OK, let's see what happens,' she said.

They sat back down and waited. Cinders's whiskers trembled as she smelled the treats. But her courage was gone and she made no move towards them.

'It's no good,' Mandy said, after twenty minutes had passed. 'She's not going to come near us now. I shouldn't have tried to touch her. We're going to have to take things more slowly.'

James looked anxious. 'But time's running out, Mandy. Sam Western's coming in three days. We *have* to have tamed her by then.'

A shiver of worry crept down Mandy's spine. Three days! Was that all? 'We'll do it,' she said resolutely. 'We just have to keep on trying.'

However, Cinders kept a wary distance for the rest of the day. Thursday slipped into Friday, and Friday into Saturday. Each day, Cinders came a bit closer to them but as soon as Mandy or James showed any sign of touching her, she panicked and fled.

'We're not getting anywhere,' James groaned on Saturday morning, as they watched Cinders make her now-familiar dash back to the nest.

'She *is* getting better,' Mandy insisted. 'She just took a treat from my hand.'

'Yeah, and then she ran away,' James said. 'What are we going to do? Sam Western's coming tomorrow.'

Mandy took a deep breath. She hated to admit it, but she was running out of ideas. 'If only we had more time,' she said.

Seemingly unaware of their mother's fear, the three kittens were milling playfully round her feet. 'At least *they're* tame,' Mandy said, picking Sweep up and giving him a cuddle. 'They'd come out of the caravan with us right now, wouldn't you?' she added to the kitten.

As she spoke, Sooty pounced on her trainer laces and began to bat them with his front paws. Mandy smiled. Over the past week, all three kittens had become increasingly co-ordinated. They could now pounce without falling over, and instead of staggering round the caravan with their heads low, they trotted, with their tails held up, looking very sweet.

Mandy put Sweep down, and the two kittens began to wrestle with each other. As well as becoming more co-ordinated, they had just started to pick at their mother's food. In another few weeks Cinders would start to wean them, and then they would be ready to go to new homes.

Mandy bit her lip. But first she and James had to get Cinders out of the caravan. The kittens were too young to survive without her. And even if they'd been older, Mandy knew there was no way she could leave Cinders in the caravan for Sam Western to deal with. No, it was up to her and James to rescue the whole family of cats. But how?

James seemed to be wondering the same thing. 'Maybe we're just going to have to catch her by force,' he said. 'Put a blanket over her like we were going to before and bundle her into the carrier. At least then we'd get her out.'

'But she'd never trust us again,' Mandy objected. She hated the idea of using force. Cinders' trust in them had grown over the last week and Mandy was afraid that if they destroyed that trust now, then taming her a second time might prove impossible.

'So what other ideas have you got?' James asked.

Mandy sighed. 'None,' she admitted. 'But we've still got the whole of today and this evening.'

Just then, they heard the noise of a car engine outside. 'I wonder who that is?' James said, in surprise.

They went to the door and looked out. Sam Western's Land-rover was bouncing over the grass towards the caravans.

'What're *they* doing here?' Mandy said as it stopped and Sam Western and Dennis Saville got out.

Dennis Saville opened the back door and let out Sam Western's two bulldogs. Fear suddenly shot through Mandy. 'James!' she gasped. 'Maybe they've come for Cinders and the kittens!'

'They can't have. Sam Western said he wouldn't come till tomorrow,' James said quickly. But Mandy saw that his face had gone pale.

Sam Western and Dennis Saville marched towards them. The bulldogs pulled on their leads beside them, panting and straining with every step.

Mandy bounded down the steps, her heart pounding. 'Why are you here?' she exclaimed as the two men drew closer.

Sam Western stopped. His eyebrows rose superciliously. 'Why am *I* here?' he queried. 'I happen to own this land, in case you'd forgotten.'

'We've come to see if those cats are still in that caravan,' Dennis Saville snapped.

'Yes, they are,' Mandy said, her mouth going dry. Seeing the menace in Dennis Saville's hard

eyes, she took a step backwards. 'But you can't take them!'

Dennis Saville ignored her. 'I told you they'd still be here,' he growled to his employer. His grip tightened on the dogs' leads. 'Shall I get them out for you, Mr Western?'

'No!' Mandy exclaimed. The dogs snarled and barked but she ignored them. 'You promised we could have till tomorrow!' she appealed to Sam Western.

'I'm going to be busy tomorrow,' he replied firmly. 'You can have until six o'clock this evening.'

'But that's not fair!' Mandy exclaimed.

'It's only a few hours' difference,' Sam Western said. He turned to Dennis Saville. 'Ring Andrew Austin and tell him to meet us here tonight. It looks like he's going to have to deal with them after all.' Turning on his heel, he marched away.

Mandy saw a look of disappointment cross Dennis Saville's face. It was clear that he would have liked nothing better than to deal with the cats there and then but he obviously knew better than to argue with his boss. With one last look at the caravan door, he followed Sam Western back up the field.

Mandy watched until the two men got back into the Land-rover. As it drove away, her legs felt suddenly wobbly and she sank down on the caravan steps. 'They're coming back tonight,' she said.

'I know,' James said in a shaken voice. He glanced at the caravan door. 'Mandy, what are we going to do?'

'We've got to get Cinders and the kittens out,' Mandy said. 'Come on, James. There's no time to lose!'

Nine

Mandy and James took the pet carriers into the caravan and tried tempting Cinders with cat food and treats, but the more they tried, the more nervous she seemed to become. She shot away from them every time.

'Please, Cinders,' Mandy begged. 'You've really got to let us catch you.'

But Cinders took no notice.

They had just reached the point of despair when there was a knock at the caravan door. Mandy froze and looked at James.

'It isn't . . .' Mandy whispered, her heart clenching.

James seemed to read her mind. 'Sam Western wouldn't knock,' he said quickly.

Realising he was right, Mandy hurried to the door. She was relieved to see it was just Wilfred.

'Your mum's been on the phone,' he said. 'She wanted to know if you were all right. She seemed surprised when I said you were still here.'

Mandy glanced at her watch. It was almost four-thirty! It was no wonder her mum was wondering where she was.

Wilfred seemed to notice her pale face. 'Is everything all right, lass?' he asked in concern.

'No,' Mandy said desperately. 'Sam Western's coming to get the cats tonight!'

'Tonight?' Wilfred echoed.

Mandy nodded. 'Can I ring Mum from your house, Wilfred? I'll have to tell her what's happening.'

'Of course, lass,' Wilfred said.

Mandy ran up to the cottage and rang Animal Ark. She quickly told her mum about Sam Western's visit. 'He's coming back at six o'clock,' she said desperately. 'And we can't catch Cinders.'

Her mum immediately understood. 'Keep trying. I'll come up as soon as I can and see what

I can do,' she promised. 'And Betty Hilder rang. She's back from her holiday and her assistant told her you had found some feral cats. Betty said she's very happy to look after them at the animal sanctuary.'

'Thank goodness!' Mandy gasped. 'At least we have somewhere safe to take Cinders and her kittens.'

'Now keep calm,' Emily Hope told her. 'If you're tense, Cinders will pick up on that and be even more frightened.'

Mandy put the phone down just as Wilfred came into the cottage.

'Mum's coming,' she told him.

Wilfred opened the fridge. 'Here,' he said, reaching in and handing her a plate with a whole cooked chicken on it. 'Maybe the cat will come for this.'

Mandy shook her head. 'Thanks, Wilfred,' she said. 'It's very kind of you but we can't take it.' She knew that Wilfred didn't have much money and that the chicken was probably his supper and lunch for the next few days.

'Of course you can,' he said, starting to cut it up into pieces.

Mandy hesitated for a moment. Wilfred's chin was set and it was clear he wasn't going to take no for an answer. Quickly deciding that she would bring him something to make up for it the next day, she took the plate gratefully.

Wilfred smiled. 'Just get those cats out before Sam Western comes back.'

Mandy raced down the field with the chicken. She kept thinking about her mum's words. *Keep calm*, she told herself.

She found James in the caravan trying to tempt Cinders with a salmon-flavoured treat. He had the two carriers open and ready, but the grey cat was just watching him warily from the nest. 'What's that?' he asked, looking at the plate in Mandy's hand.

'It's chicken to tempt Cinders with,' Mandy said. 'Wilfred gave it to me.' She took a deep breath. 'Let's hope it works.'

She crouched down and lowered the plate. As the smell of the chicken wafted into the air, the kittens, who had been playing in a corner, came trotting confidently over. Mandy offered them a tiny piece each. They smelled the titbits and then pawed at her knee playfully.

'Look,' James whispered.

The smell of the chicken had reached Cinders. Her whiskers quivered. Then, slowly, she began to creep towards them.

Handing the plate to James, Mandy took some chicken and held it out. 'That's it, girl,' she murmured. 'We're not going to hurt you . . .'

The cat crept closer until she was near enough to grab the chicken. This time, she didn't run straight off. She crouched down and ate it nearby.

While James tried to keep the mewing kittens away from the plate, Mandy offered Cinders another piece.

Cinders hardly hesitated. She took the chicken, swallowed it in one quick mouthful and then, to Mandy's amazement, stepped elegantly with one front paw on to Mandy's knees and tried to reach the plate that James was holding up.

Hardly daring to breathe, Mandy reached out and very gently touched Cinders's fur. The cat didn't seem to mind.

James glanced at her and Mandy saw he looked as delighted as she felt. Neither of them dared speak. James offered Cinders another piece of chicken. And then another, as paw by paw, the cat moved forward until she was balancing on all four paws on Mandy's lap.

Mandy's heart was racing with excitement at having Cinders so close. She forced herself to keep calm. She mustn't wreck things now. 'There's a good girl,' she whispered.

As she spoke, Cinders's eyes met hers. For one heart-stopping moment, Mandy thought that the little cat was about to turn and run. But then the last glimmer of fear seemed to leave Cinders' amber eyes. Stretching her head out, she rubbed against Mandy's sleeve and purred.

It was the moment Mandy had been hoping for all week. Feeling as if she was in a dream, she stroked the cat. Cinders arched her back against Mandy's hand and purred again. Very gently, Mandy took Cinders in her arms and stood up. Suddenly, she was sure that trying to put Cinders in the carrier would only frighten her and maybe make her panic. Mandy knew that she would have to carry her out.

'I'll bring the kittens,' James said, realising what Mandy was going to do. He scooped the three kittens up and put them into one of the carriers.

'Don't close the lid,' Mandy said, as she felt

Cinders look round to see what was happening to her babies. 'Bring them like that.'

Nodding, James picked the carrier up, ready to follow Mandy.

Mandy could hardly breathe, she was so excited. They were going to do it. They were actually going to get the cats out! Cuddling Cinders close, she pushed open the door and walked down the steps.

Suddenly, she stopped. Sam Western's familiar Land-rover and a dark blue van were drawing up by the campsite entrance.

'Looks like we got Cinders out just in time,' James said, stopping beside Mandy. They watched as a tall, burly man in overalls, carrying a cat carrier and a long metal stick with a hoop at one end, got out of the van and joined Sam Western by the Land-rover.

Mandy's legs felt shaky with relief as she looked at the metal stick in the man's hands. Sam Western was too late. The cats were safe!

The two men came striding across the grass. Suddenly Sam Western seemed to notice Mandy and James. 'The cats!' he exclaimed, stopping in front of them. 'You've got them out.'

'Yes,' Mandy replied triumphantly.

Just then, Sooty seemed to decide that he was bored with the cardboard carrier and he began to scramble out of it, his paws scrabbling as his head poked over the top of the box.

Mandy saw Sam Western turn pale. 'Keep it away from me!' he ordered.

Mandy frowned. The big man looked almost afraid of Sooty. 'He's only a kitten,' she said, as James expertly captured Sooty and pushed him down into the box.

'I don't care,' Sam Western said coldly. 'I don't want any of them near me.'

Mandy glared at him. 'Well, you needn't worry about that. We're taking them away. You won't ever have them near you again. Come on, James.'

They started to march past when suddenly the man with the metal pole spoke. 'I thought they were wild,' he said, looking puzzled.

Mandy stopped. The man's deep voice sounded unexpectedly warm. 'They were,' Mandy agreed, holding Cinders close to her chest. 'But we've tamed them.'

'Well done,' the man said. He held up the pole. 'I hate using this, but with wild cats it's often the only way.'

Mandy looked at him warily but he seemed friendly. In fact, she realised, he also seemed quite familiar. She was sure she had seen him before.

'So, have you got homes for them?' the man asked next.

'Oh, yes,' said Mandy. At least, Betty Hilder would take good care of Cinders and her family until proper homes were found for them.

'That's a pity.' The man took off his gloves and, to Mandy's amazement, he bent down to tickle Sooty's black fluffy head. 'I could have offered them a good home.'

Mandy and James exchanged astonished looks.

'My mother had her old dog put down this week,' the man went on. 'It really upset her and she says she won't have another dog. But I'm worried about her getting lonely. When Mr Western told me about the cats I thought they'd be ideal. I hoped that a family of stray cats who need lots of love and attention might be just the thing to help my mum get over Archie's death – Archie was her dog,' he explained.

'Archie!' Mandy stared at him, everything clicking into place as she realised why his face seemed so familiar. He was the man she had seen dropping Mrs Austin off at Animal Ark. 'Is your mum Mrs Austin?'

It was the man's turn to look surprised. 'That's right,' he replied. 'Do you know her?'

'I'm Mandy Hope. My mum and dad are the vets at Animal Ark,' Mandy gabbled. 'I saw her and Archie there.'

'You'll have seen how upset she was, then,' the man said. 'It's nice to meet you, Mandy. My name's Andrew.' He looked at Cinders and the kittens. 'Well, it's a pity, but if you've already got homes lined up . . .'

'But we haven't,' Mandy burst out. 'Not really. We were just going to take them to the animal sanctuary. But if you want them for your mum then you can have them.' She looked at James who nodded quickly.

'We didn't really want to take them to the sanctuary,' James said. 'It was just that they couldn't stay here. It would be great if the family could all stay together.'

'So I can have them?' Andrew Austin asked.

'Yes!' Mandy and James said together.

A broad smile broke out on Andrew Austin's face. 'That's wonderful,'

Sam Western cleared his throat behind them. 'Well, I'm glad you haven't had a wasted journey, Andrew.'

Mandy realised that she had almost forgotten that Sam Western was there. It seemed almost impossible that he had organised for someone as nice as Andrew to come and get the cats. 'You didn't tell us that you were going to have the cats rehomed,' she said to him.

'I said I would deal with them,' Sam Western replied. 'What did you think I meant?'

'That . . . that you'd shoot them or something,'

Mandy replied, feeling rather uncomfortable.

'Shoot them!' Sam Western looked genuinely astonished. 'Why would I do that? I might not want a cat as a pet but I know they're useful. They keep down rats and mice. In fact, that's why I rang Andrew. I thought he might have space for them on the farm.'

'I manage Mr Western's new organic farm,' Andrew explained to Mandy and James. 'When he found some cats here a few months ago I took them off his hands, so he thought that I might take this litter as well. But I've got enough cats now, so I thought about my mum.'

Mandy could hardly believe what she was hearing. 'But I thought you hated cats,' she said to Sam Western.

The burly landowner eyed Cinders and her kittens warily. 'I don't hate them, but I certainly don't like them,' he admitted. 'I was badly scratched by one when I was little and I've had a phobia about them since, but I wouldn't want to kill them. They're not pests like foxes or rabbits.'

Mandy felt her hackles rise at the way Sam Western talked about foxes and rabbits, but she bit back the angry words that sprang to her tongue. She had very different views on wild animals, but even she had to admit that she had judged him a bit too harshly when it came to cats.

Andrew reached into the carrier and stroked the three kittens. 'Well, I guess we had better put these little things in the van then,' he said. He looked at Cinders in Mandy's arms. 'Will she go in a carrier?'

'I'm not sure,' Mandy said. 'She's been very nervous up to now and I don't think she'll react well to being shut up.'

Andrew scratched his beard. 'Hmm. Well, I can't drive with her loose in the van,' he said. 'It wouldn't be safe.' He frowned thoughtfully. 'But I don't want to frighten her.'

'We could come with you,' James suggested.

Mandy nodded. 'That way we could hold them and they wouldn't be a nuisance.'

'Are you sure?' Andrew asked. 'I can bring you back afterwards, but won't your parents mind?'

'We could ring them from Wilfred's,' Mandy said. However, just as she spoke, her mum's Land-rover drove into the campsite. Mandy grinned. 'In fact, I can ask Mum right now.' She carried Cinders carefully over to her mother, who was climbing out of the Land-rover.

Emily Hope looked very surprised and relieved. 'So you caught her?' she said.

'Yes and that's not all,' Mandy replied, her eyes shining. 'We've found a home for them – a really brilliant home!'

Soon it was all settled. When she heard the story, Mrs Hope offered to give Mandy, James and the cats a lift to Mrs Austin's house so that Andrew didn't have to make an unnecessary journey to bring Mandy and James home.

'I can't wait to see Mrs Austin's face,' James said, as he and Mandy climbed into the Land-rover.

'I hope she's pleased,' Mandy said. Andrew had told them that he hadn't said anything to his mother about the cats in case something had gone wrong. It was going to be a complete surprise for the old lady.

They set off, following Andrew's van. As they drove through the gathering dusk, Mandy and James filled Mrs Hope in on all the details.

'So Sam Western wasn't being quite so awful as you thought,' Emily Hope said, shooting an amused look at Mandy.

'No,' Mandy said grudgingly. 'But I still don't like him.'

'Me neither,' James agreed.

'Well, somehow I don't think that's ever going to change,' Emily Hope said. 'You both see animals as individuals with thoughts and feelings, whereas Mr Western simply splits them into two groups: those that are useful to him and those that are pests.' She glanced over her shoulder and smiled at them. 'For my money, I think the world would be a much better place if more people thought the way you two do. I'm very proud of you.'

Mandy felt her cheeks go pink and she buried her face in Cinders's soft fur. 'I hope Mrs Austin likes you, Cinders,' she said, changing the subject.

'I think we're about to find out,' her mum remarked.

They had reached Twyford village. Andrew pulled up outside a row of pretty stone cottages.

'Well,' said Mrs Hope, parking behind him. 'I guess it's time to see what Mrs Austin's going to make of her new companions.'

Mandy climbed out of the Land-rover with James, both carefully holding the cat family. They hung back, feeling slightly awkward, as Andrew knocked on one of the cottage doors. Mandy held Cinders close. What would Mrs Austin say? Suddenly, she felt a little nervous. What if Mrs Austin didn't want Cinders and the kittens?

The cottage door opened and Mrs Austin looked out. 'Andrew? What are you doing here?' she asked, the lines on her face deepening with confusion.

'I've brought you a little surprise.' Her son grinned at her. 'Mandy, James,' he said, beckoning to them.

'You're the girl from the vet's!' Mrs Austin exclaimed, looking even more bewildered as Mandy stepped forward with James.

'Now, I know you said that you didn't want another dog after Archie,' Andrew began, 'so I thought that a cat and three kittens might do instead.'

'Oh!' Mrs Austin's hand flew to her mouth as she stared at Cinders in Mandy's arms. 'Oh, Andrew, no, I really don't want a pet, not again.'

Mandy's heart sank as Mrs Austin shook her head and stepped backwards. But just then, Sooty gave a high-pitched miaow and poked his head out of the top of the carrier. He looked round, his fluffy fur sticking straight up.

'Oh,' Mrs Austin said, stopping dead in her tracks, her tone changing. 'But he's adorable.'

'They *all* are,' Andrew said with a smile. As if on cue, Sweep and Smudge popped their grey-and-white heads over the top of the carrier on either side of Sooty's, and gazed round with wide, blue eyes.

'Just *look* at them,' Mrs Austin said, her voice softer.

'They need a good home.' Andrew glanced at Mandy. 'Particularly the mother.'

Mandy stepped forward. 'This is Cinders,' she said, cradling the grey cat in her arms. 'We think she's run wild ever since she was little. She was terrified of us to start with, and even now she's still very nervous.' Mandy looked pleadingly at Mrs Austin. 'She really needs someone to love her and teach her that there's no reason to be afraid of people. She needs a proper home.'

Cinders opened her mouth and mewed plaintively.

Mrs Austin's heart seemed to melt. 'Poor thing,' she murmured, going forward. 'What a life she must have led.' She looked at Mandy. 'Will she let me touch her?'

'I think so,' Mandy said, hoping desperately that she was right and that Cinders wouldn't panic.

'Hello, beautiful,' Mrs Austin said in a low voice, reaching out to stroke the cat.

To Mandy's relief, Cinders didn't move. She looked at Mrs Austin with her large amber eyes, and then suddenly gave a deep, rumbling purr.

Mandy took a deep breath. It looked like Cinders was going to accept Mrs Austin. Taking a chance, she held out the little grey cat to the old lady.

A flurry of emotions crossed Mrs Austin's face and she hesitated.

'Please, Mum,' Andrew Austin said encouragingly. 'You heard what Mandy said. Cinders and her kittens need a good home.'

Suddenly, Mrs Austin seemed to make up her mind. She reached out and took Cinders from Mandy. 'Poor girl,' she murmured. 'So you and your kittens need looking after?' She stroked the top of Cinders's head. 'Well, you'll be safe and happy here with me.'

'So you'll have them, Mum?' Andrew said eagerly.

Mrs Austin smiled round at them all. 'I will.'

Relief flooded through Mandy. Andrew's plan had worked. At last, Cinders, Sooty, Smudge and Sweep were going to have a proper home.

'Shall I bring the kittens in for you, Mrs Austin?' James offered.

'Yes, please,' Mrs Austin replied. 'And I'll sort them out a bed and some food.' Cuddling Cinders in her arms, she walked into the house. James and Andrew followed.

Mandy was just about to go in too when she felt her mum's hand on her shoulder. 'Happy now?' Emily Hope said softly.

Mandy's eyes shone as she looked at her mum. 'Very!' she said, with a smile.

Animal Ark series

1 Kittens in the Kitchen
2 Pony in the Porch
3 Puppies in the Pantry
4 Goat in the Garden
5 Hedgehogs in the Hall
6 Badger in the Basement
7 Cub in the Cupboard
8 Piglet in a Playpen
9 Owl in the Office
10 Lamb in the Laundry
11 Bunnies in the Bathroom
12 Donkey on the Doorstep
13 Hamster in a Hamper
14 Goose on the Loose
15 Calf in the Cottage
16 Koalas in a Crisis
17 Wombat in the Wild
18 Roo on the Rock
19 Squirrels in the School
20 Guinea-pig in the Garage
21 Fawn in the Forest
22 Shetland in the Shed
23 Swan in the Swim
24 Lion by the Lake
25 Elephants in the East
26 Monkeys on the Mountain
27 Dog at the Door
28 Foals in the Field
29 Sheep at the Show
30 Racoons on the Roof
31 Dolphin in the Deep
32 Bears in the Barn
33 Otter in the Outhouse
34 Whale in the Waves
35 Hound at the Hospital
36 Rabbits on the Run
37 Horse in the House
38 Panda in the Park
39 Tiger on the Track
40 Gorilla in the Glade
41 Tabby in the Tub
42 Chinchilla up the Chimney
43 Puppy in a Puddle
44 Leopard at the Lodge
45 Giraffe in a Jam
46 Hippo in a Hole
47 Foxes on the Farm
48 Badgers by the Bridge
49 Deer on the Drive
50 Animals in the Ark
51 Mare in the Meadow
52 Cats in the Caravan
53 Polars on the Path
54 Seals on the Sled
55 Husky in a Hut
56 Beagle in the Basket
57 Bunny on the Barge
58 Guinea-pigs in the Greenhouse
59 Dalmatian in the Dales
60 Lambs in the Lane

Plus:

Little Animal Ark
Animal Ark Pets
Animal Ark Hauntings
Animal Ark Holiday Specials

Animal Ark™

For more information about Animal Ark and for the latest news on the books and how you can get involved, visit the website:

www.animalark.co.uk

A division of Hachette Children's Books

Another Hodder Children's book

DOG IN THE DUNGEON
Animal Ark Hauntings 1

Lucy Daniels

Mandy and James will do anything to help an animal in distress. And sometimes even ghostly animals appear to need their help...

Skelton Castle has always had a faithful deerhound to protect its family and grounds. But Aminta, the last of the line, died a short while ago. So when Mandy and James explore the creepy castle the last thing they expect to see is a deerhound – especially one which looks uncannily like Aminta . . . Could it possibly be her? And what does she want with Mandy and James?

Another Hodder Children's book

CAT IN THE CRYPT
Animal Ark Hauntings 2

Lucy Daniels

Mandy and James will do anything to help an animal in distress. And sometimes even ghostly animals appear to need their help . . .

Mandy is haunted by dreams of a mysterious cat. Could it be because she is worried about Bathsheba, the vicarage tabby who has run away? Or does the strange, stone-coloured cat of her dreams have something to tell her?

Another Hodder Children's book

RABBITS ON THE RUN
Animal Ark 36

Lucy Daniels

Mandy Hope loves animals more than anything else. She knows quite a lot about them too: both her parents are vets and Mandy helps out in their surgery, Animal Ark.

Farmer Sam Western is threatening to destroy the rabbits in a nearby warren, as they keep going on to his land to eat his crops. Mandy, James and their friend John Hardy are desperate to save the hungry rabbits. The question is, how? Then Mandy has a radical idea: to relocate them. But will it work?